"You and I are to marry."

Had he said that he planned to ride a dinosaur down to Independence and back, or perhaps catapult himself high enough into the air to swat down the sun—that would not have been any more astonishing.

"I... What?"

"You are the key," Cayetano Arcieri, self-styled *warlord* of a country she'd never heard of, who had earned his place in *blood and fire*, assured her.

Delaney's throat was upsettingly dry. "I feel pretty sure I'm not."

"You are the lost heiress to the crown of Ile d'Montagne, little one," Cayetano informed her. "And I have come to take you home."

He said that the way something as over-the-top as that should be said, really, all ringing tones and *certainty* and that blaze in his burnt gold eyes. Delaney thought the corn bowed down a little, that was how impressive he sounded.

But all she could do was laugh.

The Lost Princess Scandal

Swapped at birth...but now the secret is out!

Delaney Clark has grown up on a farm in the Midwest. The idea she has royal blood is absurd to her...until Cayetano Arcieri tells her the shocking truth. She is the long-lost princess of Ile d'Montagne, and if she accepts his hand in marriage, he can offer her a crown and a passion more incendiary than anything she's ever imagined. But will that be enough for Delaney to accept?

Find out in *Crowning His Lost Princess*, available now!

When Princess Amalia of Ile d'Montagne discovers she's not a princess at all, her priority is finding a place where she can hide away and plan a new future. She does *not* expect to be sharing that place with the unforgettable Spaniard from her past, Joaquin Vargas...or for their illicit chemistry to still burn as brightly as it ever did. But is it hot enough to scorch through the barriers keeping them apart?

Find out in *Reclaiming His Ruined Princess*, coming soon!

Don't miss this sexy and dramatic duet from *USA TODAY* bestselling author Caitlin Crews!

Caitlin Crews

CROWNING HIS LOST PRINCESS

Recycling programs
for this product may
not exist in your area.

ISBN-13: 978-1-335-56957-8

Crowning His Lost Princess

For questions and comments about the quality of this book, please contact us at CustomerService@Harlequin.com.

Harlequin Enterprises ULC
22 Adelaide St. West, 41st Floor
Toronto, Ontario M5H 4E3, Canada
www.Harlequin.com

Printed in U.S.A.

USA TODAY bestselling, RITA® Award—nominated and critically acclaimed author **Caitlin Crews** has written more than one hundred books and counting. She has a master's and PhD in English literature, thinks everyone should read more category romance and is always available to discuss her beloved alpha heroes. Just ask. She lives in the Pacific Northwest with her comic book artist husband, is always planning her next trip and will never, ever, read all the books in her to-be-read pile. Thank goodness.

Books by Caitlin Crews

Harlequin Presents

Chosen for His Desert Throne
The Sicilian's Forgotten Wife
The Bride He Stole for Christmas

Pregnant Princesses

The Scandal That Made Her His Queen

Royal Christmas Weddings

Christmas in the King's Bed
His Scandalous Christmas Princess

Rich, Ruthless & Greek

The Secret That Can't Be Hidden
Her Deal with the Greek Devil

Visit the Author Profile page
at Harlequin.com for more titles.

CHAPTER ONE

DELANEY CLARK RAN the back of her hand over her too-hot brow, frowning at the clouds of dust in the distance.

Someone was coming up the long dirt drive toward the rickety farmhouse and the tired old barns and outbuildings. In the middle of the afternoon. And that was unusual, because no one was expected.

She glanced over toward the old farmhouse, where her mother had raised her the way she'd been raised in turn. The way Clarks had raised their children here since the land was first settled. But she didn't need to walk inside from the vegetable garden to see what Catherine Clark was doing or whether she was expecting anyone. Her mother didn't get out much any longer, and any visits were planned well in advance— usually through Delaney, who hadn't planned a thing for her this week.

Delaney's confusion only grew when she

saw what looked like a fleet of gleaming black SUVs roaring up the quiet lane.

Pickup trucks would have been one thing. This was Kansas. Right smack in the middle of the great prairie. Pickups were the preferred mode of travel, because everything was farmland or farmland adjacent. She would have been surprised to see a line of pickups barreling her way, too. But she could come up with a number of reasons why her neighbors might show up together.

She could not, however, think of a single reason that five extremely fancy-looking SUVs should come out to the farm at all. She couldn't even imagine who might be driving them— or where they would get such vehicles this far from anywhere. Her closest neighbor was a fifteen-minute drive away. The nearest town around was Independence, but calling it "close" was pushing it. It was half a day's drive south.

Well, missy, I expect you'll just have to wait and see what's going to happen, won't you? came a familiar wry voice inside her. Her beloved grandmother's voice. Delaney still hadn't fully accepted Mabel Clark had passed. It had been some five years ago, but the pain of it still walloped her when she least expected it.

Even now, with the memory of her grandmother's scratchy voice in her head, she could feel the hit of grief. She tried to shake it off.

Delaney walked across the yard, wiping the dirt off her hands on the bib of her worn and torn overalls. She wasn't dressed for company, but she supposed that folks who turned up out of the blue shouldn't expect much more than the dirty overalls she was wearing and the faded bandanna on her head. She stood there, frowning a little, as the gleaming black vehicles came to a stop before her, kicking up dust in all directions. She counted five in total.

And for a moment, she thought that maybe they'd realized their mistake. Maybe they were all peering out their dramatically tinted windows at her and realizing they'd taken a wrong turn somewhere.

Because nothing happened.

It was just Delaney, out beneath the endless bowl of a Kansas sky, corn stretching in all directions. It was a pretty day, not too warm or too cold, and she supposed if she had to stand around in her own yard waiting to see who'd taken it upon themselves to show up here today, she ought to be grateful there wasn't a rainstorm. Or a tornado.

Thank you, Grandma Mabel, she said in her head.

She was grinning a little when the door of

the vehicle that had stopped in the center of the other four opened.

By this point, Delaney could admit, she'd let anticipation get the better of her.

But it was only a driver. Though that, too, was fascinating. Who had a *driver*? She supposed she'd become her mother's driver, in these last few years since Catherine's arthritis and heart trouble had robbed her of so much. But she did not make her mother ride in the back seat. Nor did she wear a uniform. Unless her overalls counted.

Somehow Delaney knew that her overalls did not, in fact, count. Not to the sort of people who rode about in fleets and had uniformed drivers to open up their doors.

And it was an otherwise ordinary Tuesday, so she found herself far more interested in who, exactly, those sorts of people might be than she might have otherwise. She was really bemused more than anything else when the driver nodded at her as if she was exactly who he'd come to see, which was both laughable and impossible, then opened the back door of the SUV.

Some part of her was expecting trumpets to sound.

But there was still no particular sound, so there was nothing to distract her from the way the breeze danced in from the fields, or the sound of the wind chimes that made her mother happy, and then, there before her, the most beautiful man she had ever seen in her entire life...*unfolding* himself from the back of the SUV that seemed entirely incapable of holding him.

Because what could possibly hold...*him*?

He was otherworldly. Almost alien, so little did he belong here in the middle of this rolling prairie, where the farmhouse and the red barn stood exactly as they had for ages and yet, she was sure, had never borne witness to anything like him.

Even the tornadoes would find it hard to top this man.

She knew exactly where the sun was above her, and yet Delaney felt certain that it had shifted. The better to beam its golden light all over this man. As if the sun itself wanted nothing more than to highlight him as best it could.

Delaney found she understood the urge. She felt it herself, everywhere. When she could not recall a single other time in her twenty-four years that she had ever had any kind of reaction to any kind of man. The boys she'd grown up with had been nice enough. They still were. And if she'd wanted, she had always suspected she could have gotten close to one of them and settled down the way so many of her high school classmates had.

It had never really occurred to Delaney to do anything of the kind. Because there was the farm. There had always been the farm. There was Grandma, and her mother, and Delaney took very seriously the fact that she was the last Clark. This land would be hers—was already hers in all the ways that mattered—and while she didn't intend to farm it alone the way her mother had done since Delaney's father had died before she was born, she also knew she had to make sure she picked the right kind of man.

She had yet to find a man around here who came close to her idea of the right kind.

It had never crossed her mind that the reason for that might be because none of them were *men*. Not like this man was.

As if he was redefining the term.

Delaney was always solid on her own two feet, planted right where they belonged in Kansas soil, and yet she actually felt dizzy as she stared up at the man before her. As if he was doing something more than simply standing there next to that obnoxiously glossy SUV that still gleamed as if the country roads hadn't dared get any dirt on it.

It wasn't that she thought the creature before

her was the right sort of man. It wasn't like that, no matter that her body was doing all kinds of bizarre things. Too hot. Too cold. Fluttery, for some reason. As if he was so beautiful that human eyes were not meant to behold him.

Maybe she was coming down with the flu.

Besides, she doubted very much a man like *this* even knew what a farm was. He likely looked down the not inconsiderable length of his own body and saw nothing but dirt. Delaney had no use for such people.

She told herself that. Repeatedly.

Still, she couldn't seem to bring herself to look away from him. Maybe it was the loving way the sun fell over him, calling attention to the crisp black suit he wore that should have made him look as if he was attending a funeral. Yet it did not—or not the sort of funeral Delaney had ever attended around here, anyway. Maybe it was the way he held himself that made her think of the neighbors' prize bull. Never quite at rest, always rippling with that ferocious power right beneath the surface that could erupt at any moment…

Though she associated the sort of suit he was wearing with men in magazines, always too angular and wee to her mind, he wasn't either of those things, either. He was powerfully built, a symphony of lean muscle in a tall frame that made her breath feel a little short.

She had the sudden, strange conviction that this was a man who was well used to people looking up at him the way she was.

He was wearing dark glasses, but as she stood there gaping at him, he shifted them from his eyes. He did not shove them on the top of his head, or even on the back of his head, the way folks often did around here. He slid them into the lapel pocket of that suit of his, a small, simple gesture that made clear the breadth of his sophistication. She couldn't have said why. Only that it was as obvious as the width of his shoulders, the power in his chest, all the rest of him cast in stone and dark glory.

And Delaney should have laughed at herself for even thinking something like that. *Dark glory.* It was so melodramatic. It was so unlike her.

But then, it was almost too much to look upon his bare face. It was almost *too much.*

It was as if he'd been carved, not born. As if he'd been sculpted in a fury, bold lines and a forbidding palette. She thought of stone again, immovable. The harnessed power of great, wild animals. And some kind of hawk, too, fierce and commanding as he peered at her.

The man was…a lot.

"Wow," Delaney said, the word coming out of her mouth of its own accord. "Who are you? Are you lost?"

That was the only thing that made sense. That he was lost, out here in the prairie in his conspicuous caravan to God only knew where. That he'd turned in to ask for directions, perhaps—though that was hilarious in its own way. Since he looked like a man who would *know* where he was, always. As if he was his own compass in all things.

She was vaguely aware that other doors were opening, and other people were coming out of the gleaming vehicles, but she couldn't seem to look away from the man before her. She felt as if she was caught, somehow. As if he was deliberately holding her where she stood. There was something about his burnt gold gaze that nailed her to the spot. And though it wasn't even warm, she could feel herself heat up—even as a strange shiver worked its way from the nape of her neck all the way down her spine.

Dark glory was the only term that fit.

"You are called Delaney Clark," the man said.

"I am," she replied, because it seemed important that she answer him immediately. And only when she had did it occur to her that he hadn't actually asked her a question.

That had been a statement. As if he already knew her when she knew she most certainly did not know *him*.

That should have been a huge red flag, but all Delaney could seem to think about was *dark glory* and the way he spoke. That was certainly no Kansas accent. It was as if his words had a particular spice to them, and the way he said her name—

Get a grip, girl, she ordered herself. *Before you start drooling on the man.*

She was embarrassed at the very idea.

But she didn't step back.

"I see it," the man pronounced. And Delaney was aware, then, that he was making some kind of declaration. More, that all the people he brought with him were making murmuring noises as they gazed at her, as if that declaration meant something to them. Something intense. "The cheekbones. The mouth. And of course, the eyes. She has a look of the Montaignes."

Again, there were more murmuring noises of assent. And awe, if she wasn't mistaken. And Delaney was still standing there in her overalls, with dirt all over her, allowing this strange moment to drag on. Because she didn't know quite what to do. Or what to say.

Or maybe because this man was too darkly beautiful and it turned out she was a silly little farm girl after all. That was how she felt, which was novel in its own right, because she had never been *silly*. Surely she could come up with something to say that wasn't *dark glory* or the neighbors' bull.

"Who *are* you?" she asked again.

Not exactly an improvement, though not as bad as it could have been. Delaney realized how dazed she was when the men flanking him stepped forward. Because she hadn't even seen them fall into place like that. But there they were, clearly…*bodyguarding* him.

In response, the man himself…barely moved. He did something with his head. Maybe inclined it slightly. Maybe shook it? But either way, the men froze on either side of him, as if he'd stopped them with his own hands.

"I am Cayetano Arcieri," he replied.

And then waited, as if his name itself tolled across the field like deep and terrible bells, calling down storms from above.

But it was still the same old Kansas sunshine. Delaney blinked. "I can tell that I'm supposed to recognize that name."

The man before her was hard and fierce, yet the way his brow rose was nothing short of haughty. "Do you not?"

"Well. No. I can't say that I do. I'm guessing you're not a salesman. I doubt you're here to see about the tractor, which is a pity, because it's nothing short of poorly these days. And to be honest, I'm pretty sure I would remember that name if I'd ever heard it before." She shook her head sadly. Because she actually was sad that she was who she was and always had been—and that, therefore, there was no way on earth this man could possibly be looking for *her*. It felt a bit like grief, but that was crazy. "I thought you were lost, but now I think maybe you have some bad information."

He no longer looked haughty. Or not entirely haughty. A weather system moved over his face and what was left was a glinting thing that made her feel entirely too warm.

His hard mouth curved. Slightly. "If you are this Delaney Clark, and I can see that you are, I am afraid, little one, that I'm in exactly the right place."

No one had ever called Delaney *little one*. She had the sense she ought to have been offended.

Yet that was not, at all, the sensation storming around inside of her.

"I really don't think so," she said, because it felt critically important to her that she set the record straight. It didn't matter that every part of her *wanted* to be this man's *little one*. She would have to investigate that later and ask herself some hard questions. Probably. But she couldn't cope with extending this misunderstanding.

She had the oddest conviction that humoring this man not only wouldn't work, but that going along with him only to discover that she was not the Delaney Clark he was looking for would...*bruise* her, somehow.

And merely being in his presence felt bruising enough.

The more he looked at her, the more she began to feel as if the burnt gold of his gaze was somehow...*inside* her. She could feel the flames. And that delirious heat.

Cayetano seemed impervious to the dust beneath him, the breeze, the typical Kansas spring carrying on all around. He seemed to grow broader and taller the longer he stood there before her...and Delaney had never considered herself a whimsical person.

It was difficult to be too whimsical on a farm. There were too many chores.

And yet that was the only word she could think of as she looked at this man. *Whimsy.*

Except a lot hotter.

"I come from a country called Ile d'Montagne," Cayetano said. He paused as if he expected her to react to that, so she nodded. Helpfully. His mouth—a thing of wonder itself, stark and sensual at once—curved faintly once more. "It is a small place. An island in the Mediterranean to the north and east of Corsica. And it has been ruled for many centuries by false kings and queens."

Delaney felt as if she was outside herself. Nodding along while this man who could have stepped out of a Hollywood movie talked to her of kings and queens. *Kings and queens,* of all things, as if *royalty* was something he thought a great deal about. In his day-to-day life. So much so that there was a difference between false and un-false kings and queens.

Maybe she was actually still in her vegetable garden. Maybe she'd toppled over and hit her head on her loop hoe and was dreaming all of this.

That made a lot more sense than this conversation.

With this impossibly magnetic man.

Out here in the yard, talking of *royalty* and Mediterranean islands.

"For almost as long, there has been a rebellious faction," Cayetano told her. "The mountains that form the spine of the island have been contested since the first false king attempted to claim it. Just because a man comes along and calls a bit of land his, that doesn't make it so. There have been skirmishes. What has been called a civil war or two, but for that to be the case, all involved would need to be citizens. Subjects. When those who fight do not consider themselves either. Between these conflicts there have also been long stretches where those who reject the false kings merely...wait."

"Wait?" Delaney repeated. Hoping she sounded like something more than a mere parrot.

But what else was there to do but squawk?

"Wait," Cayetano agreed, his gaze dark and intent. "Have you never heard the proverb? Wait long enough by the river and the body of your enemy floats by."

That seemed to take an unnecessarily dark turn, in her opinion, in an already notably violent little tale this stranger was telling her. Out here in the yard where she should have been alone with her plants the way she was every other day.

"I can't really speak to rebellious factions hunkering down in contested mountains," Delaney said. Nervously. Her hands suddenly felt like they might betray her in some way. So she shoved them into the pockets of her overalls. "Or waiting by rivers. You do know that this is *Kansas*, don't you? We don't really have mountains. Though there are some big rocks."

Was it her imagination or did Cayetano move

closer? Whether it was or not, she found she was having trouble breathing, and instead of being alarmed by that...

She kind of liked it.

Obviously she was not well.

But still, she couldn't seem to move.

"For centuries, my people have waited to claim what is theirs," Cayetano told her, and his voice was low now. Almost quiet. And yet it was as if all the fields in all directions went still. As if the sky paused, the better to listen. To *wait*. "For an opportunity. A chance. My grandfather negotiated our current peace, which has held far longer than anyone thought might. Yet still we believed that any chance we might get to reclaim what is ours could only come with bloodshed."

Bloodshed.

And...there it was at last. That alarm that Delaney should have been feeling from the start. It washed through her in a torrent then, so electric she was sure she could feel every hair on her body stand on end.

"I'd like to come down firmly against bloodshed, if that's an option," she said, as carefully as a person could when talking about...whatever it was they were talking about here. This very serious nonsense the man with the burnt gold eyes seemed so intent on sharing with her.

"I am a warlord," the forbidding man before her told her. "I earned my place in blood and fire."

"Metaphorically?" Delaney asked with a nervous little laugh.

No one echoed that laugh.

The men arrayed behind him were stone-faced. Cayetano himself appeared to be fashioned *from* stone.

"I have found a far better way to reclaim my ancestral lands than any war," he told her, his gaze never wavering. "A foolproof plan, at last."

"Oh, good." Delaney was beginning to feel something like lightheaded. Or maybe it was more of that dizziness. "That sounds much nicer than bloodshed."

The look on his face changed, then. And if she hadn't been so overwhelmed she might have thought that, really, it looked a lot like amusement.

Assuming a man like this was capable of being amused.

"That depends on how you look at it," Cayetano said. Distantly, Delaney registered the laughter of his minions, indicating that they were capable of it. "You and I are to marry."

Had he said that he planned to ride a dinosaur down to Independence and back, or perhaps catapult himself high enough into the air to swat down the sun, that would not have been any more astonishing.

"I...what?"

"You are the key," Cayetano Arcieri, self-styled *warlord* of a country she'd never heard of, who had earned his place in *blood and fire*, assured her.

Delaney's throat was upsettingly dry. "I feel pretty sure I'm not."

"You are the lost heiress to the crown of Ile d'Montagne, little one," Cayetano informed her. "And I have come to take you home."

He said that the way something as over the top as that should be said, really, all ringing tones and *certainty* and that blaze in his burnt gold eyes. Delaney thought the corn bowed down a little, that was how impressive he sounded.

But all she could do was laugh.

CHAPTER TWO

THIS WAS NOT the response Cayetano had expected.

An offer of marriage from him should result in exultation and gratitude, not laughter. He could think of any number of women who would have fallen to their knees and praised the heavens had he indicated he wanted a second night, much less a lifetime.

This woman was baffling.

More to the point, she was not what he'd expected, either, and he had pored over all the photographs his spies had gathered for him. He had looked for every possible clue to determine that she was, in fact, who he hoped she was. She should not have been a surprise in any way. On balance, she was not—the pictures his men had obtained of her were accurate.

But that was all they were. A picture could only show her features. It could not capture the warmth of her. The way she drew the eye without seeming to try. The brightness that seemed to light her from within—when he had long since accepted that the Montaignes were a clan of darkness and bitter cold, every last one of them.

Not this lost one, it seemed, with all this American sun in her hair.

And more, in her very eyes somehow, so that that famous Montaigne blue was neither cold nor fierce, but bright enough to make a man think of little but the kinds of summers other men enjoyed. On tropical beaches far away from the concerns of a contested throne.

He had seen her standing in the dirt, dressed like a peasant—and despite these things, had been shot through with a hunger unlike any he had ever known. He had sat in his car, waiting for the intensity of his hunger to pass, yet it had not.

Even now, her peals of laughter still ripe in the air between them, it only grew.

Cayetano blinked at the direction of his own thoughts. Since when had he considered himself nothing but a mere man? He had never had that option. Not for him the call of flesh and sin. Not for him the comforts of oblivion. His entire existence had been honed and focused to a hard shine.

And yet here he stood in this foreign place,

thinking of sunshine and excess, and the sweet oblivion of flesh and desire.

But the unexpected lost heiress of Ile d'Montagne was still laughing. As if, truly, she had never heard anything more preposterous than what he had told her. As if anything he had said to her was funny.

As if he, Cayetano Arcieri, sworn enemy of the Montaignes no matter the two generations of uneasy peace, was given to telling *jokes.*

Cayetano could see the way his men began to scowl at the insult, but he waved them back as they started forward. He told himself he was letting her go on merely to note how long it took her to collect herself, and then to understand the discourtesy and disrespect she showed, but he had the sneaking suspicion that, actually, it was simply to watch all of that light dance around her—

You must stop this, he ordered himself grimly. *There is more at stake here than your* hunger.

"It is a lot to take in, I grant you," he said stiffly when she wiped at her eyes.

"It's just so silly," she said as if she was agreeing with him. "What a story. First of all, I'm not lost. I'm right where I'm meant to be, right here where I belong. And there are certainly no crowns involved. Or *princesses.*"

And that set her off again, tossing her head back to laugh straight up toward the endless sky.

Cayetano could admit that he had not given this part of his mission as much thought as the rest. Finding her had been the hard part. It had taken time and patience, when he was famous for ignoring the first when it did not suit him and exhibiting very little of the second when he pleased. The task before him had been immense and overpowering.

He'd had to believe the impossible. Then prove it.

That he had done so beat in him, a dark drum of victory, even now.

It was, perhaps, not unreasonable that he had thought collecting her would be the easy part. What he wanted to do was simply toss her over his shoulder, throw her in the car, and start the journey home. He wanted to focus on what came next. How and when he would finally disrupt the line of succession and take back what had been stolen from his people so long ago, not so much breaking the peace between the factions in his country so much as obliterating the need for it. Both the peace and the two factions, in one fell swoop.

It had never occurred to him that he would have to *convince* his Princess to reclaim her place.

Though diplomacy was not his strong suit,

Cayetano endeavored to make himself look… nonthreatening. Understanding and inviting, if such a thing were possible.

He did not think he achieved anything like it.

"Perhaps this is too much to take on faith," he said, trying to sound sympathetic. Though the edge he could hear in his own voice suggested he was not successful. "But you're not required to believe me. The science speaks for itself."

"The science?" She repeated the word, then started laughing again. "What science could there possibly be to lead a *warlord* to a quiet old farm in the middle of nowhere? I'm telling you, I think you took a wrong turn. Maybe back in whatever mountains you're from. I'm not the Princess you're looking for."

But the more she insisted, the more he saw the truth of her parentage. The absence of doubt. The deep belief in her own discernment above all else, when surely it should have been clear to her that a mere farm girl could not possibly have access to the same information as a man of his stature. It should have been glaringly apparent.

Cayetano was not conversant in Americans or farm girls, it was true, but he felt sure that without the Montaigne blood in her veins, this one would have quaked before him, as was only right and proper.

"It did not begin with science, of course," he told her, shifting as he stood.

He was not accustomed to having his commands and wishes dismissed, but he was also aware—on some distant level—that it would not serve his cause to take this woman against her will. It would only muddy things, and he needed clarity. Rather, he needed to appear to act with clarity and sensitivity, the better to fight the right battles.

Probably it would not kill him. He attempted a reassuring smile, but she only frowned.

"There were whispers," he told her, still trying to exude something other than his usual forbidding intensity. "There are always whispers around any throne, but perhaps more so in Ile d'Montagne, where the ruling family has been contested for so long. Mostly these are rumors that come to nothing. Just malicious little tales told to pass the time between spots of civil unrest. In this case, someone began telling a story that Princess Amalia was a changeling, almost from the moment of her birth."

His lost princess blinked. "A changeling. Like in a fairy tale."

She sounded doubtful. And if he wasn't mistaken, that look on her face was a clear indication that she did not find him a trust-worthy source.

But he didn't have time to revel in that novelty.

Delaney was wearing a pair of coveralls that should have offended him on every level, so common were they, marking her as some kind of farmhand when she would be his bride. But she stood in them with such confidence that he noticed her lush form instead. There were freckles across her nose, but they only drew attention to the perfection of her cheekbones. And her hands looked capable and strong, not merely delicate appendages suitable only for the hefting of fine jewels. To think—all this dirt, all these fields, and she was nonetheless the true heir to the kingdom.

She pleased him more than he'd dare imagine.

As did the fact that whether she believed it or not, she would be his.

"There's no particular reason that such a fairy story should come to my attention," Cayetano told her. "I do not make a habit of listening to the dark fantasies of bored aristocrats. Yet in this case, the story did not die out quickly the way the most outrageous usually do."

"At least we can agree that the notion of

changelings is outrageous," Delaney offered. Almost helpfully.

Did she intend to be provoking? He could not tell, so he pushed on. "I could not get the idea out of my head. And the more I considered it, the more it seemed obvious to me that Princess Amalia was not who she pretended to be. Dark-haired and light-eyed, yes. But too many other curiosities that had never before appeared in the Montaigne line throughout history."

"I think you'll find that's called genetics."

This time Cayetano had no trouble recognizing that she was, almost certainly, provoking him. Or, at the least, defying him in what small way she could.

He opted not to react to these affronts the way he normally would. He inclined his head instead. "When there arose an opportunity to test the genetic material of the current Princess against that of her supposed mother, I had no choice but to take that opportunity."

"You took blood samples from princesses and queens?" Delaney shook her head as if she hadn't meant to say that. "This is an entertaining story. Really. I always had a soft spot for fairy tales. But the more outlandish this all gets, the less and less I believe it. And I didn't believe it to begin with."

Cayetano waved a hand as if it was nothing, her disbelief. He would not tell her, then, the lengths he and his men had gone to. The risks they had taken. The potential penalties had they failed.

None of it mattered, for they had not failed.

"But the tests were conclusive," he told Delaney quietly. "Princess Amalia of Ile d'Montagne bears no genetic relationship to the Queen. She is not Queen Esme's daughter."

"Okay." Delaney wrinkled up her nose. "You do know that people are complicated, right? There could be any number of reasons for that."

"Indeed. And we have explored them all. But I will tell you the most astonishing thing. Are you ready to hear it?"

"Is it more astonishing than all the other things you have said?" she asked.

Rather aridly for his tastes. And yet his hunger to taste her continued unabated.

"Queen Esme suffered from a particular cocktail of ailments while pregnant," Cayetano told her with a quiet ferocity. "Because of them, she was taken to a specialist hospital in this vast country of yours. A city with the unlikely name of Milwaukee."

"Yes," said Delaney, her eyes narrowing. "I was also born in Milwaukee. As were a great many other people, I think you'll find. This is absurd."

But Cayetano looked behind her. An older woman had come to the door during their conversation and was standing there on the other side of the screen, listening to him tell this story.

Not just listening, he corrected himself. Frozen into place.

He pushed on. "There were twelve babies born in that hospital on that particular day. Only two of them were girls. One was the Crown Princess of Ile d'Montagne. The other, a farm girl from Kansas."

"And you think…what?" Delaney demanded. She was frowning even more deeply now, which Cayetano hoped meant she was also beginning to take the truth on board, however unpalatable to her. "That somehow, a princess and a perfectly normal girl from Kansas were—"

"Switched," came the older woman's voice. She pushed open the screen and stepped through it onto the porch. Her expression was taut, but her eyes were bright. "There in the hospital. On the third day."

Cayetano already knew he was right, but that didn't prevent the surge of triumph that raced through him then. A deep and satisfying roar from deep within, because the throne of Ile d'Montagne was in his grasp at last.

He had succeeded.

Finally.

He studied the girl as she turned, jerkily, as if her mother had taken a swing at her. And had made contact.

"Mama?" Her voice sounded too soft now. Almost plaintive. "What are you talking about?"

"I knew," the older woman whispered, loud enough to carry across the cornfields. There was a fierce look on her creased face. "I knew they brought me the wrong baby. I said so, didn't I? The nurses all laughed. They told me I was a new mother, that was all. Drunk on hormones, no sleep, and whatnot. But I knew."

"Mama?" Delaney's voice was thicker now.

More panicked, Cayetano noted, and that couldn't be helped.

"For a time I thought something was wrong with me," the older woman continued, her voice stronger with each word. Only then did she look at the girl she'd raised into a woman. The baby that wasn't hers. "And it didn't matter, because I loved you. With everything I am, Delaney, switched or not. But the switch explains too many things that have never made sense. That you can carry a tune, for one thing. There's not a Clark stretching back into the old country who was anything but tone-deaf."

Delaney was full-on scowling now. "Mama, this is ridiculous. Babies aren't switched in hospitals. You're as likely to have a child snatched by the fae folk and I hope we all know *that* is pure fantasy."

"I know what I know, Delaney. No matter how addled you think I've become."

"I don't think you're addled, Mama," Delaney retorted. "But I know you're weak. This sort of melodrama can't be good for you."

"I know what I know," the older woman repeated, looking mutinous. She nodded at Cayetano. "And so does he."

"There's an easy solution," Cayetano interjected, at his ease now, because as far as he was concerned the truth was already out. "We can perform a quick genetic test here and now. No need to debate *what-ifs*. This is not about feelings, you understand. It is about facts."

And it was a fact that the way his future wife looked at him then should have set him alight. Cayetano found he liked the burn of it.

Something in him shifted. Readied itself.

He liked that, too.

Delaney's fierceness faded a bit when they moved inside, her expression changing into something closer to apprehension. Cayetano sat there in the tidy, cozy sort of living space that looked the way he supposed he'd imagined an American farmhouse would. Having never entered one before. When he would have said he took in very little foreign media.

But this room felt familiar to him just the same, down to the stitched sampler on one wall.

He stared at it as his doctor administered the tests quickly. The results were nearly immediate. The man cleared his throat and made the expected announcement, there in the homespun room.

And then there was no further need to argue the point.

Delaney Clark was not related to her mother. She was, however, possessed of nearly fifty percent of the DNA of Queen Esme of Ile d'Montagne.

The facts did not lie.

"This can't be happening," Delaney said. More than once.

In a voice that sounded less and less like the one she'd used at first outside.

"As I have told you," Cayetano said mildly, for he was at his ease now. All that was left was convincing her to do what he, for one, already knew she would. Because it could be no other way. "It is only science."

He found himself unprepared when her bright blue eyes shifted to him, wide and accusatory. "It is not just science," she whispered. "This is my *life*."

Cayetano did not have it in him to understand the lure of farmland when kingdoms awaited. But then again, who more than he understood the connection one had to the place they called home?

He settled himself in the chair that, for all it looked worn and tired, likely rated as among the most comfortable he'd ever sat in. He attempted to arrange his features into something…understanding.

Failing that, he attempted to look less forbidding.

Because now that the tests had been administered, he needed to present himself as less of a warlord, if possible. And more of a bridegroom.

He wasn't sure it sat easily on him, but he attempted it all the same.

"It is time for a new era in Ile d'Montagne," he told her quietly, holding that blue gaze. "For too long it has been a country torn in two. For too long it has been brother against brother, no one safe, no one trustworthy. There is no way to build a future in these conditions. There is only war and uneasy treaties in between. There is only loss, fighting, and generations of waiting for the next blow. It must end."

Delaney was breathing roughly, but she did not speak. Cayetano looked over at her mother, sitting near her on the couch, but the old woman had her gaze lowered.

"You may think that I have come to find you to advance my own interests above all else," Cayetano said gruffly.

"Because that's why you came, didn't you?" she asked, and something flashed in her gaze before she, too, dropped her focus to her lap. "You want that throne."

"I am the leader of one half of my country, it is true." Cayetano was not ashamed to admit this. Still, he did not love the way his words seemed to hang in the air between them. "I wish to marry you not only because it will grant me access to the throne, though it will. But because you represent the other half of my country and I wish our union to unite all of Ile d'Montagne's people."

"Your people, you mean," she said, more to her lap than to him. "People who have nothing to do with me."

"I do not want revenge, Delaney. I want renewal. My country needs it. And you are the only one who can make this happen." She did not respond to that, though her chest moved as if she was breathing heavily. "I don't know what you think it is a princess does."

She lifted her gaze to his. It was not a friendly look, but something in him sang nonetheless. And that hunger inside him bit deeper. "I have never given the matter the faintest shred of thought. I have been too busy planting. And farming. And a great many other tasks princesses are not known for, I'd guess."

Cayetano waved a hand. "It is irrelevant in any case. What matters is what you and I will do. We will create a bright and gleaming future. Your blood and mine will pave the way to the future, together. Gone will be the bitter, bloody factions of the past. Together, you and I will remake the world." It was a ringing speech and all the better because he meant it—though he had prepared it before meeting her. He had prepared it for the idea of her. He couldn't have said why that felt wrong, now. He shook off the strange notion. "All you need do is say yes."

She did not even need to do that, but this was America. Cayetano paid little attention to the doings of the place as a whole, but even he knew that Americans deeply prized their sense of freedom, however elusive it might prove in reality. No need to tell his farm girl that her acquiescence was merely a formality. There was no earthly reason to tell her that he, the warlord of the Ile d'Montagne hills, would be only too happy to toss her over his shoulder and handle the situation in the time-honored fashion of his people.

He did not think she would react to the news well.

It was another indication of how sheltered she was, out here surrounded by her corn and her vegetables. It had yet to occur to her that a man on a mission that was intended to remain wholly peaceful did not turn up with a battalion.

Though he did find that he was suddenly far more intrigued by the notion of his people's marital wedding practices, which he had always considered archaic, than he ever had been before.

Delaney stared at her hands for a long while, though the ragged movements of her chest gave away her continued rough breathing. She lifted her gaze again, her blue eyes seemed almost tortured, and Cayetano felt…

Not regret. Not quite. But something in him twisted, all the same.

"I wish you the best of luck, then," she said, almost solemnly. "But this sounds like your fight, not mine. Even if I was remotely interested in some far-off place I've never heard of, it would be impossible. I belong here. This is my home."

She held his gaze as she said it. She looked

at him steadily, as if wishing him on his way even now. She was dismissing him, he thought with some amusement, and that was certainly not the way he was normally treated.

It was so unusual that it was almost…nice.

"Delaney," he began, trying to sound…reasonable.

"There's no possible way," she said, shaking her head as if the matter was decided and she had moved on now to be faintly sorry about it. "I can't even consider it. Maybe you noticed the whole farm outside. It can't take care of itself."

The older woman stirred herself then, there on her end of the couch she shared with Delaney. Her eyes were grave as she gazed at Cayetano, then back at Delaney. She looked as if she was taking her time coming to a decision. Then she nodded, slightly.

"I'm needed here," Delaney said, her voice urgent. And cracking around the edges, to Cayetano's ear, the longer she looked at her mother—who wasn't truly her mother. "You can't do this alone, Mama, you know that. You *can't*."

The old woman smiled, and something in it made Cayetano's neck prickle.

"I do know that," she said softly, and the softness was not for him. Her gaze had been shrewd when she took him in. The softness was for Delaney, and she smiled when she turned to the daughter she'd raised. And loved, he saw, just as she'd said. "But nonetheless, Delaney, I think you should go."

CHAPTER THREE

DELANEY COULDN'T STOP shaking. She couldn't remember ever actually *shaking* before in her life, and now it was as if she was little better than a leaf in a swift wind. She was actually *trembling*.

And she would have hated that she was so weak, but she couldn't seem to focus on her body or the things that were happening in it. Not beyond noticing what was happening.

Not when her world had fallen apart.

Cayetano murmured something and left the room, taking his men along with him. She hardly knew the man who had turned up here and set everything spinning madly out of control, so she shouldn't have been surprised to see him show a little compassion. But she was anyway. Or maybe it was the opposite. Maybe it was a performance of deep cynicism, because he had somehow known what her mother would say. Maybe he was simply, politely, leaving the two of them to talk now that all his *facts* were laid out.

Not that it mattered, because the shock waves from her mother's surprise statement were still rolling through *her*. And Delaney knew without having to ask that for all his apparent compassion—or whatever it was inside a man made of stone—he was not going far.

She couldn't think about that, either. Or any of the implications when she didn't hear any car engines turning over outside.

Because now was simply her and her mother, here in this room, where she'd spent the whole of her life. Where she knew every picture in every frame. Where she'd played on the floor as a child, there on the thickly woven rug. Where she and her mother—*not your mother,* came that terrible voice inside her—sat in the evenings and worked on their sewing, their knitting, and other projects while the light was good.

This farm, this house—this was her *life*.

How could her mother possibly tell her to go?

"You can't think that any of this is real," Delaney said furiously. "No matter what it says on a test that he could easily have doctored—"

"I know that you're upset," Catherine said. And she suddenly seemed imbued with the strength Delaney hadn't seen in her in ages. It made her heartsick that it was only now. Only under these bizarre conditions. "I understand. I'm upset, too."

Delaney couldn't keep herself on her end of the sofa any longer. She moved toward her mother, reaching out without thought and making a little sobbing sound when her mother grabbed her hands.

It was hard to tell who held on tighter.

"Listen to me," Catherine said, her voice as fierce as her grip. "You are my daughter. In every way that matters, *you are my daughter.* I took you home from the hospital. I loved you. I raised you. We're not debating whether or not you are mine. You are, Delaney. *You are.*"

"But you said…" Delaney croaked out, horrified when she realized the water splashing on her hands was coming from her eyes. Clarks didn't cry. Clarks didn't make scenes. Clarks endured. But this Clark felt as if she'd already been carried away in a tornado. "You told him…"

"I had a funny feeling," Catherine said quietly. "And was quickly told it was my hormones, that was all. Over time I would sometimes remember that feeling, when you would sing, perhaps. Or when I would think about the fact that you don't have the Clark chin. All Clarks have the same pointy chin." She tapped the end of hers, round and stubborn. "You don't even have mine. Still, these are little things. I love you, Delaney. I find myself interested in meeting the child I bore in my body, I won't lie. But that will never change my love for *you*."

Delaney couldn't let herself think about that other child. That *princess*, if Cayetano was to be believed. And how could she possibly believe a word he'd said? How could her quiet life have anything to do with *princesses?* It made no sense.

She knew about corn. Not thrones.

"Even if it's true," she said, after a moment—though she didn't think it was. But Catherine clearly did. "Even if somehow it's actually true, that doesn't mean that I need to go off somewhere with this man. This *stranger.* It certainly doesn't mean I should *marry* him."

"Weddings don't necessarily happen overnight," her mother said, an odd gleam in her gaze. "No need to rush into anything, I would say. But I think what we have before us is an opportunity, Delaney."

"An opportunity for what?" Inside, she thought, *to question everything? To find out I'm not who I thought I was?* She could have done without the opportunity, thanks.

All she'd ever known, all she'd ever wanted, was the farm.

"I know you love this land," her mother said quietly. Almost as if it hurt her to say. "But I have agonized over it. As my own strength wanes, I've watched you try to work with your own two hands what it took my father and a full set of workers and family to maintain. How can you possibly stand up to it? How can anyone?"

"It's Clark land," Delaney protested. "I'll find a way. That's what Clarks do."

"I'm an old woman now." And Catherine sounded firm now. She patted Delaney's hand in the way she'd always done. A quiet *chin up, child.* "I have tended this land since I was little more than a girl. Sometimes I think I'd like to live in town, in the time I have left. It would be nice to walk somewhere, if I wanted. Be easy, if I wish. Sleep in late and leave the cows to do their business with someone else."

Delaney's heart was kicking at her, some whirl of fear and panic and too many other dark things she couldn't name. Or breathe through, really.

She made herself focus on her mother, not whatever was happening inside her. "Mama, if this is how you feel, why have you never told me?"

"How could I tell you?" Catherine asked quietly. "You've already given up so much for this farm. You are young, Delaney. You shouldn't be here, isolated and away from everyone. You have more in common with a vegetable patch than people your own age. It's not natural. And it's not good for you."

Delaney sat back, pulling her hands away. "But you think some stranger showing up and saying he wants to spirit me off to play some sort of political game is better? How is that natural?"

"What kind of life will you have if you never leave the farm?" Catherine retorted. "I could never think of a way to tell you what I thought you should do. You have always been so determined. And you never asked. But it seems fate has taken care of it, doesn't it? You have a birthright, Delaney. You already know what this one looks like. Why don't you go and see what this new one is about?"

"Because I don't want to go!" Delaney cried, and she didn't care if Cayetano with his burnt gold warlord eyes could hear her. "I don't want to go anywhere!"

Her mother—*because she is still my mother, I don't care what that test said,* she told herself—reached over and patted her hand again. She had that canny look about her that Delaney had always rued. It was too much like her grandmother. It always led to truths she'd have preferred to ignore. "Is it because you truly don't wish to go? That's fine. No one will make you go anywhere if you don't want to go. I don't care how many cars he has."

"Thank you," Delaney said in a rush—

But Catherine held up a hand. "I wonder, though, if it's more that you're *afraid* to go?" She shook her head. "Because if that's the case, my dear girl, then I'm afraid I will have to insist."

It took Delaney two days to answer that question.

And she wasn't happy about it. Any of it. She spent forty-seven hours talking herself around and around in circles. And a lot of those hours succumbing to emotions unbefitting a person who had been raised in the Midwest.

Emotions were for high-strung coastal types. Midwesterners were made of sterner stuff. Salt of the earth, in point of fact. She would pull herself together as quickly as possible, reminding herself that *salt of the earth* did not mean sobbing into her pillows.

But then she would remind herself that she wasn't made of anything Midwestern at all. Because the DNA test didn't lie, much as she wished it did. She'd researched it. Delaney was a good Kansas girl who'd been raised up right on a farm—but now she was a *princess*.

It felt *wrong,* that was all. There was no other word for it.

Except embarrassing.

A man had showed up in the yard one day and the life she'd thought had been built on a solid foundation, generations deep, turned out to be nothing more than a row of dominoes.

None of them hers.

The truth was, she blamed said man for those dominoes. She'd researched him, too. It didn't take much. It seemed that most papers' coverage of Ile d'Montagne and its current rebel leader were nothing short of fawning. All papers, in fact, save those actually in his country.

Delaney held on to that like it was evidence.

Or maybe because it was all she had to hold on to.

Because everything else seemed to be rolling downhill, and fast.

Catherine was moving into town. She intended to sell the land to the neighbors, to keep the farm in good hands. But when Delaney had argued that she should stay and oversee the move and the sale and the unfathomable life changes she hadn't even realized her mother desired, Catherine had waved her away.

You've been seeing to me for far too long, she had said, again and again, until Delaney was forced to accept that she really, truly meant it. *It's time you go out and live.*

So this was Delaney living.

Against her will.

The fleet of glossy SUVs came back up the lane far too early that morning. And this time, only Cayetano emerged.

They stared at each other, he from beside the muscular vehicle that, if anything, looked glossier and more pristine than before. She stayed where she was—on the step where she had taken herself after saying her goodbyes to her mother, red-eyed and cried out and wondering how on earth she was supposed to *live* through this.

And how exactly she could prove that she'd lived enough so that she could come back home.

Assuming there was any *home* to come back to, without the farm.

Not to mention, she isn't your mother, came that same insidious voice inside her, forever telling her things she didn't want to hear. Not her grandmother's voice, sadly. She would have welcomed Grandma Mabel's observations, however dry.

This particular voice sounded a lot more the way she imagined gold might.

If it was burned half to ash.

"You do not look excited, little one," Cayetano said from his place beside his enormous SUV, in that voice of his that seemed to change the weather. She felt a breeze that hadn't been there before dance over her skin.

"That's because I'm not," she replied, scowling at him for good measure. "Would you be excited to be torn from everything you know and forced to march off to a foreign country because someone thinks your blood will...*do* something?"

"Focus less on blood," Cayetano suggested, with a faint curve to his hard mouth that she ordered herself to stop looking at. "And more on what pleasures await."

Delaney didn't much care for the way the word *pleasures* burst open inside her. Like a water balloon against the side of the old barn.

"If you're talking about the whole marriage thing, forget it." And she couldn't understand why she wished, immediately, that she hadn't said that. That she hadn't heard the word *pleasures* and mentioned the marriage that was never going to happen. It was...unseemly, somehow. She hurtled on, her cheeks hot. "My mother thinks that I need to go and see my birthright. I keep telling her I'm happy with the one I already have, but she insists."

"Are you refusing to marry me?" Cayetano asked, but not as if the prospect made him angry. There was none of that haughtiness. Or even a particular sense of the threat he posed. Instead, he looked as if her refusal amused him.

It was disconcerting.

"I am." She said it as bluntly as possible, so there could be no mistake. "I am absolutely refusing to marry you. Because the very idea is absurd. I don't know you."

And again, that little tug in the corner of his mouth sent a terrible heat, far more intense than the flush on her cheeks, cartwheeling through her. Once again this man felt like a fever.

She ought to tell him to do something about his infectiousness, but she didn't quite dare. Or maybe the truth was that she liked all that cartwheeling.

"Allow me to tell you something about me, then," he said, as if he could see her turning cartwheels inside. As if he knew. "I love a challenge, Delaney. I have yet to meet a challenge I couldn't get the best of. Better you know that now."

That was an unambiguous warning.

And there was a flash in his gaze that made the skin over her bones seem to draw tight. She was suddenly aware of herself in a way she never had been before. Right there on the porch steps of the comfortable old farmhouse, she felt...*lush,* somehow. Her breasts ached and felt heavier than before. There was a shivery sensation that started at the nape of her neck and wound its way ever lower, down the length of her spine, spreading more of that shimmering lushness as it went. Strangest and most wonderful of all was that between her legs, she felt hot and bright.

Maybe it wasn't her fault that she'd never paid much attention to the boys she'd grown up with. Maybe the problem was that none of them had ever looked at her and made her feel like a whole weather system.

As if, that voice inside her whispered, *the moment you met this man you became someone else. Not because of your blood. But because he changed you from a farm girl into a princess with a glance.*

And she *felt* it. She felt different, down deep in her bones. As if no matter what happened, even if she returned here the way she wanted to, she would never be the same.

But Delaney also knew, in a flash of insight that felt like truth no matter how odd, that she must not, under any circumstances, start talking to this man about *weather.* Whatever she did, she needed to keep how profoundly changed she felt to herself.

"I expected your mother to see you off," Cayetano said, and there was a note in his voice that made her wonder how long she'd been standing on the porch like this. *Gazing* at him.

It must have been at least a minute or two, because he was no longer standing beside his vehicle. He was standing in front of her. She was sure that if she inhaled, his scent was there, a faint hint of spice and heat that made her... *want* things.

Mostly Delaney wanted to lift her hand to her cheeks, to test the heat there, but she thought that would be a dead giveaway. And she was not going to tell him about *her* weather issues. No matter how close he was.

She scowled at the bag Catherine had insisted she pack, there at her feet. "We've already said our goodbyes. We don't need to perform them out here for you to see it."

"I understand," he said smoothly. "Parting must be difficult."

It might kill her, actually—but Delaney refused to cry anymore. And not where Cayetano Arcieri could see it. She focused on him instead. Today he was wearing another one of those suits that made her reconsider her stance on suiting altogether. Because on him, there was no denying it looked good. Even out here on the farm, where he should have looked silly wearing such formal clothes.

Nothing about this man was silly.

But, no matter how good he looked, he was still the reason that she was being forced to do this. She picked up her bag with very little grace, and then practically bit her tongue to keep from reacting when he simply...took it from her hand. Then dropped it back on the ground.

"My woman must necessarily carry many burdens," he told her in that way he had, like he was inscribing stone as he spoke. "Such is my lot in life, and thus hers. But she does not carry her own luggage as long as I am alive."

He moved to usher her toward the vehicle, lifting a finger in the direction of one of the other tinted windows. And that lifted finger was a call to action, clearly, because another car door opened immediately. When she glanced back over her shoulder, her bag was being loaded into one of the other SUVs.

But there was no time to concentrate on such practical matters, because Cayetano was closing her inside the vehicle he'd exited. The interior was dark. Cool. And noisy—

Until she realized that the racket was inside her. It was the thunder of her pulse through her veins. It was her heart, deep and loud.

And when Cayetano swung into the deep seat beside her, that didn't help.

I've made a terrible mistake, Delaney thought in a panic.

She only realized she'd said that out loud when Cayetano shifted in the leather seat beside her. He reached over and took her hand in his, a nurturing sort of gesture that astonished her. She was…floored. So much so that she couldn't seem to do a thing save freeze in response.

He didn't squeeze her hand the way her mother might. In fact, the longer he held her fingers in his, the heat of his palm skyrocketing through her, the less nurturing she found the whole thing.

She expected him to say something. To make another one of those statements of his, so matter of fact, as if the world would arrange itself before him as he willed it. Simply because he wished it.

But he said nothing. It was only when she heard her own breath come out in a long sigh, from somewhere deep inside her, that she recognized the uncomfortable truth. The simple act of him holding her hand was…calming.

It wasn't only calming. It was a great many other things and a significant number of weather changes, but above and around and in all of that, it was *calming*.

Nothing could have confused her more. How could anything about a man so elemental be calming? How was it possible?

It took her a long time to lift her gaze to his, but when she did, she caught her breath all over again.

Cayetano's burnt gold eyes blazed. And there was something about the hard stamp of his mouth that made everything inside her feel overly fragile. Perilous, even. As if she wasn't sitting down in plush leather but teetering over the side of some great height, so high she didn't dare look over to see the ground that must surely be rushing toward her—

He dropped her hand, but it was not until he pulled a buzzing cell phone out of his pocket that she understood why. Even then, she had the most bizarre urge to protest. To reclaim his hand. To touch him as if this was something she did, leaping into strange cars with strange men who wanted impossible things from her. Dark, overwhelming things involving thrones and vows, no less.

And maybe a weather system or two, came that voice.

This time sounding amused, the way her grandmother would have been if she'd been around to see her usually unflappable granddaughter so...*flapped.*

Cayetano called out something that made the car begin to move, and then directed his attention to his call, stretching out his long legs before him as he sat back.

And Delaney could not understand a single word he said, rapid-fire, like poetry at top speed. French, she thought, though she'd only ever heard French spoken on television. Or no, possibly Italian. Because she sometimes watched cooking shows.

But she couldn't help feeling, now that the urge to protest the loss of his attention was mostly gone, that his attention being directed elsewhere felt like a reprieve.

She needed that as the SUV turned around, then headed back down the lane. She needed to be herself again, even if it was for the last time.

Because this car—this man—was taking her away from everything she'd ever known.

You can't really want to sell the farm, she had protested.

I would have sold it after your grandmother died, Catherine had replied with that steel that had reminded Delaney of when her mother hadn't been the least bit fragile. *It was all you had. But I want you to have more, Delaney. You deserve more.*

It's because I'm not yours, she had dared to say. Earlier this very morning, standing stiff and feeling unwelcome in the same kitchen that had once felt like an extension of herself.

You are mine, Catherine had replied fiercely. *You will always be mine. But I will not let this cursed farm stand between you and an opportunity like this.*

I have no interest in being some kind of trophy wife, Delaney had protested. *You should know that.*

Then don't become one, Catherine had replied. She had even laughed, like a fist to Delaney's heart. *Be whatever and whoever you wish to be. Just promise me you will give this adventure a chance, Delaney. That's all I ask.*

She'd had no defense against that. Against her mother's heartfelt plea—even if Catherine wasn't technically her mother. In all the ways that mattered, she was and always would be. How could she say no? Until Cayetano had showed up here, she had assumed she would never leave the farm. And so she'd often been wistful, watching far-off places on television, trying to imagine what it would be like to sink her toes deep into exotic white sand beaches. Or climb distant mountains.

Or just…*be somewhere else,* where no one knew anything about her unless she told them.

And every time Catherine had caught her being wistful, Delaney had always assured her that she was all about the farm. Always and forever about the land. Because what good was wistfulness when there was a growing season to consider?

Someday, her mother had liked to say, *you're going to see the world, Delaney.*

And they'd both laughed, because the only world Delaney had ever been likely to see was on television.

Until now.

Just promise me you'll give it a chance, Catherine had said this morning.

I promise, Delaney had whispered, because how could she do anything else?

And then she'd sobbed when her mother had hugged her, as if it was the last time. As if this was a kind of funeral. Hers.

Giving up something when you don't know what it is isn't much of a sacrifice, Grandma Mabel had told her once in her usual crisp, knowing manner. *And the truth is, it's only the choices that hurt a little that make us any better.*

Well, this hurt.

A lot.

Delaney could repeat those things to herself over and over. She could even accept, somewhere deep down, that they were true, and maybe—in time—the acceptance would bring her solace.

Maybe she was setting off on an adventure

and the real reason she was so unnerved was because, deep down, she was as excited as she was apprehensive. Maybe she thought admitting that was a betrayal.

She didn't know.

But the grief sat on her all the same, heavy and thick, until the farm was out of sight.

CHAPTER FOUR

THAT THE LOST Princess of Ile d'Montagne might not wish to marry him after he had spent all this time tracking her down had never crossed Cayetano's mind.

He found the very notion of her refusal preposterous. For it was normally he who was forced to crush expectations, maintain boundaries, and make certain that none of his lovers ever got the wrong idea. He had never intended to marry. He rarely intended to spend more than a night or two with a single woman—it was too tempting for some of them to imagine that it meant something it could not.

Because Cayetano was not meant to be like other men. He could sample pleasure, and he did, but his was a life of duty. Responsibility. And the great weight of his people's destiny.

It was only his country that could inspire him to take vows, and he had made those vows long ago. It was only his country—and the sure knowledge that because his sacrifice was for the island, he would never commit the sins his own parents had. His father by dying too soon and too badly and leaving a mess in his wake. His mother by losing herself and her purpose entirely.

He didn't like to think of such things. It was too tempting to allow his memory to take him to places far too painful. When he had been a boy, powerless and far away from all the things that mattered to him. Cayetano had vowed then that he would never be so powerless again.

Never for him the betrayal of his duty for love, no matter what it looked like. He would not make the mistakes his parents had. He would not allow emotion to poison him as it had them.

Ile d'Montagne came first. Always.

He had comforted himself with the knowledge, as his obsession with finding the lost Princess grew, that he was not focused so intently on the *woman.* That would be unacceptable. That would put him on a level with his mother and he could neither accept nor permit such a thing. Cayetano was fixed on her *function*, that was all.

As they drove away from her farm, he told himself that keeping her functional so that she could play her part was all that mattered. And was why he had…held her hand, as a lover might. That was why he had attempted to give her comfort.

He, who had been bred for war.

Never in his life had he been so pleased to take an irritating call that he barely had to pay attention to as the car pulled away from the farm. He should never have taken hold of her hand in the first place.

It was better that he pay less attention to the woman beside him. Better that he make certain his armor was in place and the vows he'd made to himself when he was young still held true, no matter how perfectly her hand had fit in his.

Or how that hunger within him raged on.

As a set of his advisors tried to one-up each other on the call, Cayetano found himself toying with old memories, frayed at the edges, as they made it to the private airfield. Memories he preferred to believe he had excised. The last time he had seen his father, so distant and remote, the way a warlord ought to be in Cayetano's estimation—far above the petty concerns and mawkish sentimentality of normal people, surely. And then later, lost beneath the weight of his dismay and powerlessness after his father's death, chafing at the restriction of his age. Unable to go home and take his rightful place.

He had vowed to himself that once he was old enough, he would make himself the perfect warlord.

No emotions allowed.

But there was no use reliving the past. What mattered was that he had wrested back control of his people. And together, they had all moved on.

There was enough history to fight over when it came to the crown. Cayetano did not care to add his family's history to the list. Especially when he had handled it all.

The way he handled everything.

As an instrument of his people, stripped free. He concentrated instead on the future. He loaded his precious cargo onto the jet that waited at the airfield, prepared to take the lost Princess back home. Where a new life awaited them. Both of them, and his country, too.

Finally.

His men dispersed as they boarded, taking up their usual positions throughout the plane. Cayetano led Delaney to the area that functioned as a lounge. And watched, with some amusement, as she looked around, her eyes wide.

"Have you ever been on a plane before?" he asked, amused by the notion of such newness. But then, why should a farm girl fly?

"Never." She blinked, taking in the quiet luxury that surrounded them. And finding it overwhelming, if the way she curled her hands into fists at her sides was any indication. "But I'm pretty sure that any plane I might have gone on would not look like this."

"You may wish to brace yourself," Cayetano said, almost idly. "Because you're a princess, Delaney. You're going to have to get used to the royal treatment."

The look she threw him then would have been comical, had she not looked so genuinely horrified.

"I don't know a thing about that," she protested. "I don't *want* to know."

But he was already getting to know this woman, whether she liked it or not. And having nothing to do with his body's response to her. Or almost nothing, he amended. He had studied her in advance and meeting her in person had only added to his arsenal. He knew her tells. Like the mutinous look in her blue eyes just now. And a set to her jaw that spoke of stubbornness, not overwhelm.

He found it cute, really. He liked to watch her spark. Because whatever stubbornness she might possess, it was of no matter in the long run. And certainly no match to his. It might even serve her well in the days to come.

She had wrestled crops, perhaps, in this wholesome life she'd found herself in by accident. But it wasn't who she was. And he could assume, from the redness of her eyes, that she had a wealth of feelings about her change in circumstances. But Cayetano had been born to a calling. And he had been shaped since was small to be nothing short of the weapon that could finally topple a throne and restore his kingdom.

She could be as stubborn as she wished. It would change nothing.

But he knew better than to say so now.

He took his time settling himself in his preferred chair, then indicated that she should take the one opposite him. And was not surprised when, instead, she sat on the leather couch that put her farther away from him. As far as she could get while remaining on the same plane.

It was hard not to admire these little rebellions, however futile. At heart he would always be the rebel he'd been raised to become. Even now that he had secured a different future for his beloved island.

"I sympathize with your situation," he told her when they were both seated, though only he was anything like relaxed. And it was not entirely untrue. "It cannot be easy to learn that you are not who thought you were."

She blinked a few times, rapidly, then scowled at him. "If you sympathize, you wouldn't have turned up out of the blue, dropped a bomb, and then taken advantage of the mess you made to push your bizarre agenda."

"You misunderstand me." He inclined his head. "Sympathetic as I might be to your plight, that does not change the facts."

He had grizzled old advisors who dared not argue with him. But this little farm girl crossed her arms, tilted her chin up higher, and dug in. "The facts as you see them, you mean."

Cayetano smiled. Patiently. "Facts do not require a certain perspective to be true, though I know many people these days like to pretend otherwise. Facts, you will find, are true whether you like them or not."

She only sniffed. "You can keep making pronouncements all you like. It's not going to change the fact that regardless of what any test says, there's not one single cell in me that is in any way *princess material*."

He did not say what he could have. That the only material that mattered was her DNA, it was inarguable, and her feelings were irrelevant. Somehow he knew that would not land well—and it seemed almost churlish to belabor the point when he'd already won.

"I understand that this is difficult for you," he

told her as the plane began to taxi. He saw her look of panic, quickly hidden, and the way she reached out to grip the arm of the sofa. Though she never made a sound. Not his Princess. "I admire your bravery, little one. To charge headlong into the unknown takes courage, whatever your reasons."

"I don't really think I'm charging anywhere," she told him, still arguing though her voice was a bit higher than before. "For one thing, I don't have a passport. So at some point or another, you're going to find that your big plans are destined for—"

But she stopped midsentence as he drew an American passport out of his breast pocket. "I took the liberty of arranging one for you." He flipped it open so she could see that it was, in fact, a picture of her.

She did not look pleased at his forethought. "How is that possible?"

He lifted a shoulder. "You will find that a great many things are possible when you are willing to pay for it."

Delaney's scowl deepened. "I don't understand. I thought you were some ragtag band of freedom fighters, off in the hills somewhere. How do you have private jets? And enough money to do things that shouldn't be possible?"

The plane leaped into the air then and she let out a soft gasp that she clearly tried to muffle.

Cayetano extended her the courtesy of ignoring it. He furrowed his brow as if lost in thought when really, he was allowing her a few moments to look out the window and pretend she wasn't panicking.

"The Ile d'Montagne crown has spent a great deal of time and effort attempting to dismantle the wealth and status of those they like to call rebels," he said when the plane leveled out and her cheeks took on some color again. "And for a long time, they succeeded. We used to have to hide ourselves and the truth about our capabilities. There were sanctions, embargoes, and cruel laws that targeted only our part of the island. We built a castle hidden in the side of a mountain so that only we would know it. Many of these things changed with the last peace accord. We no longer have to pretend. And because my family has always taken care to hide our resources outside the reach of the grasping Montaigne family, we did not have to build ourselves up from scratch."

He knew this personally. He had been one of those resources—deemed too precious to the future of the country to be permitted to grow up there, no matter how peaceful things were meant to be in his lifetime.

Cayetano could still remember with perfect clarity his first trip to cold, drizzly England. His father's gruffness as he was dropped off at boarding school, left in the care of his ever-present and always watchful guards. Because he was an easy target. Everyone agreed. There was a security in the fact his whereabouts were known by the international press, but all it took was one overambitious Montaigne to shrug and decide the global condemnation was worth it and he'd have been done for.

His visits home had always been more stealthy. It was always best that the Queen not know precisely where the rebel faction's hope for the future was at any given moment, particularly not on the island where she claimed her sovereignty. It was healthier.

And he was as educated as any Montaigne princeling had ever been when he finally returned home to claim his birthright at twenty-one. To wrest it back from his unscrupulous would-be stepfather and try to find it in him to forgive his mother her betrayal. He still tried. Because he understood loneliness, after all his years in the north. He had never taken part in the heedless, reckless shenanigans of the careless students around him in the places he studied. Not Cayetano. When he was not studying, he was fighting. Or learning all the things he might need to know should he do what no one else had done and break, once and for all, this Montaigne stranglehold on his island.

Because the peace might still hold, but everyone knew that the Montaignes could renege on their part at any point.

Cayetano had been raised to act as if there was no peace. As if he was as ancient as the wrong done to his people, a warlord from long ago, prepared to battle with his hands if that was required. Any time he might have been tempted to waver, he needed only to remind himself of those who waited. His people, who waited and prayed and supported him, even when he was far away on that cold island so unlike his own.

A pity that his own mother had not managed to do the same.

But he had handled her as he handled everything. It was his duty. And Cayetano Arcieri always, always did his duty.

"And when you speak of the grasping Montaigne family, you mean…my family," Delaney said, snapping him back to the present. "*My* grasping family, according to you."

"I do not know if you are grasping or not." Cayetano kept his voice mild despite the unpleasant memories kicking around inside him. "How could I? But I can think of no other way to describe the work our false kings and queens have done for centuries."

"If it is so terrible, and has gone on for so long, how do you hope to change it?"

He studied her for a moment. He did not expect such cynicism from an American. Were they not a country raised on hope? Yet he could see the flush in her cheeks and suspected she spoke not because she was particularly hopeless, but because she was out of her depth.

Cayetano told himself he was not imagining other ways he could put that flush on her lovely cheeks. He told himself his hunger for her had abated. Even as he had to adjust the way he sat.

"I do not believe that a lie can flourish when faced head-on by the truth," Cayetano told her, with perhaps more ferocity than necessary. "And you, little one, are the embodiment of that truth."

"I'm just a farm girl," she said, but her chin lowered a notch. "I don't embody anything. Unless it's Kansas dirt."

"But you see, the DNA you care so little about will do it for you." Cayetano was keeping his voice soft, but still she sat up straighter. He reminded himself that she was not one of his people, used to ages of struggle. Moreover, she was not one of his men. She would likely respond better to honey than salt. It was on him, then, to find some honey within. However scant. "It matters not what you believe, or who you think you are. Your blood tells the truth."

"Maybe it's different where you're from," she said with a quiet hint of steel. He liked that, too. He wanted to explore all her possibilities, when it had never occurred to him that she would interest him like this. It would take getting used to—he had only thought of what she would do for his people, not what she might do for him. Though his sex was interested in little else. "But I've never found truth treated as much more than an opinion."

"I am Cayetano Arcieri," he replied, with his own suggestion of steel. Or perhaps it was more than mere suggestion. "In some places, the very hint of my opinion is treated like a commandment."

She blinked at that, but she didn't alter her expression. Or attempt to curry his favor in any way. She only gazed at him, looking faintly censorious.

That, too, was new.

"That isn't the least bit healthy," she chided him. *She* chided *him*. "If that's true."

And Cayetano had the strangest urge to truly laugh then, when he was not given overmuch to the practice. Still, he found he wanted to throw back his head and let go...when he never let go.

That wasn't who he was. Far too much was riding on this for levity—

But still, the urge was there, making its own ruckus inside him.

"The door to the left leads to a guest room," he told her when the urge within him subsided. He indicated the door he meant with a nod. "Feel free to make it your own during the flight. If you find you need anything, you can find me either here or behind the door on the right."

And if he had been an insecure man in any regard, the face she made then would have cut him straight through.

"I can't think of any reason I would need you," she retorted.

Much too quickly.

And he waited until she disappeared behind her guest room door, locking it loudly and ostentatiously, to grin.

But the grin soon faded and once it did, he could hardly recall how it had happened in the first place. He called in his men, and tried to get his head back into the business of this thing they were doing here. This glorious thing, this marvelous enterprise, that would finally restore his kingdom.

His life's work, the work of so many lives before his, *this close* to fruition.

Yet he soon found that when he should have been thinking critically, planning out how best to launch his lost little princess on the world—with the proof of who she was so there could be no debate, and the inevitability of her ascension, and thus his, secured in the minds of all the world—all he could think about was the scent of her hair. Like sweet almonds. Or the strength in that hand of hers that he'd held in the car. It was no princess's hand, that was for certain. Her nails were cut low and he had felt the work she'd done all these years in the roughness of her skin.

He should have been thinking of strategy. Instead he thought, *It suits her.*

And more, he found himself wondering how those hands would feel on his skin. His sex.

Cayetano, who preferred his women draped in silks, round and lush, found himself growing almost uncomfortably hard at the very notion. Of a peasant's hand on a princess, but then, he knew the truth about her. Even if she did not.

There was nothing common about her at all.

He nodded at something one of his men was saying in support of Delaney.

"She will make us a fine queen," he agreed.

Yet what he thought was, *She will make me a fine wife.* Having nothing at all to do with her strategic importance and everything to do with that hunger in him that only seemed to grow—even as he sat with his men. The people who depended upon him to be rational.

He tried to call on that rationality now.

"Her unusual upbringing is a gift, I think," he said now. "As we know, the Queens of Ile d'Montagne are not known for their work ethic."

"Their treachery, more like," one of his men said with a snort.

"And pretenders to the throne all the while," growled another, setting off the predictable calls for the end of the reign of the Montaignes, once and for all.

The calls had a different flavor this day, Cayetano thought. Now they were so close to their goal.

Yet he wasn't basking in their triumph the way he should have been. Instead, he found himself thinking about how, when his men had made their discreet inquiries and pretended to be looking for farmland to buy, the first thing anyone had to say about Delaney Clark was how hard she worked. She had put her heart and soul into it, as if it had been her mission since birth to save that farm. Most of her neighbors thought that if anyone could, it was her.

Imagine, what could a woman like that do for my country? he asked himself.

Or for him, not that he chose to accept he needed anyone.

But as a warlord turned king, he would. He would need a queen who could support him, not defy him. Instead of a woman like his own mother, so bitter and resentful. Focused on the past, on avenging any and all historic wrongs, and never what might come next unless it suited her ambition. It was a fine line to walk. History must never be forgotten. He lived that truth. The history of his people and the island animated all he did. But it was far too easy to sink too deep in it and risk losing everything.

This had been his mother's downfall. Therese Arcieri had imagined herself a kingmaker. Her family's roots were sunk deep into the island, just as the Arcieris' were. And she had imagined that after Cayetano's father died, her favor alone could elevate the man of her choice to the position of warlord.

But Arcieris did not sit idly by while other men attempted to rule their people.

Even if standing up against his own mother had killed something in him, something he doubted he could get back. Something he'd told himself could not matter when his country was on the line.

Cayetano had taken his rightful position by the ancient rites. He had defeated his mother's lover with his sword, and then had showed him mercy. His people had risen up and called him warlord when he was little better than a lad. A mere twenty-one, but he had stepped into his destiny.

He had showed that same mercy to his treacherous mother, little though she deserved it. And she might have railed against the manner of his mercy, but yet she lived. When he would have been well within his rights to show her the harshest possible justice.

Many had called for it. Some still did.

But on some level, Cayetano understood her. He too thought only of the country. How could he blame Therese for doing the same?

Liar, came a voice from deep inside him. *You cannot bear to part with your last remaining parent. You are as sentimental as anyone.*

That snapped Cayetano back to the plane he flew on and the men who surrounded him. Because he was no pathetic child. He had never been given the opportunity.

His mother lived because he was merciful. She remained locked away because she deserved to live with what she'd done.

Sentimentality had nothing to do with it.

But when his men left he settled in on the bed in his own state room for the rest of the flight. And he found himself thinking that Delaney Clark was nothing like Therese Arcieri, the would-be Queen of Ile d'Montagne. For one thing, Delaney wanted no part of this. She'd had no wish whatsoever to leave that farm.

To his way of thinking, that already put her head and shoulders above any other pretender to the throne. For anyone who aspired to rule should be prevented from doing it, Cayetano had long believed. He would include himself among that number, save for one thing. He did not want the throne for his vanity. He did not want the power for its own sake.

He wanted what he had always wanted. What he had been brought up to want. And had then interrogated from every possible angle while he'd studied abroad, looking for the lies inside himself.

In the end, it was simple. He wanted Ile d'Montagne to be a country torn asunder no more. He wanted his country whole. And that could not be accomplished, no matter his strength, by a simple show of force. All that would do, if successful, was switch the positions of the two factions. He needed Delaney to bring the country together.

For as long as there was a Montaigne on the throne, the royalists in their seaside villages would fall in line. But only if an Arcieri was also on the throne would his people from the mountain valley do the same.

This was the opportunity his people had been waiting for since antiquity.

She was.

Cayetano would do everything in his power to make certain he finally delivered what no other ever had.

And possibly enjoy his little farm girl more than he'd expected he would, while he was at it. Maybe that was a good thing. Maybe that would make this all the sweeter.

Because she might not think she wished to marry him.

But Cayetano knew she would.

CHAPTER FIVE

DELANEY WOULD HAVE denied it if asked, but she did feel the faintest stirrings of something like excitement hours later as she peered out the window during the plane's descent, much as it shamed her to admit it.

Surely she should have been in tears, so far away from home and with no home to return to anyway, with Catherine resolved to sell.

Not that it was her home anyway, really, since she wasn't a Clark after all.

She'd spent the whole of the flight hiding away in her room, giving herself a crash course in all things Ile d'Montagne. She'd done some research in the days since Cayetano had appeared in the yard, but then, she'd mostly been looking for things to refute Cayetano's claims. Or *him*, if that was even possible. Instead she'd seen pictures of a princess who looked…not unlike her, once she looked beyond the fancy dresses and actual tiaras. It had been too much for her, fast. She'd found she had a deep and instant aversion to looking any further into the actual human woman who she'd been *swapped with* in a Milwaukee hospital.

Because Princess Amalia hadn't chosen this, either.

It was like someone walking on her grave. It had made Delaney shiver.

But she'd sucked it up on the flight today. She'd repressed that shiver. And she'd done a deep dive into the road not taken these last few hours.

She'd looked at pictures of the Princess she wasn't. She'd studied the other woman's face, and she didn't think she was kidding herself when she saw the Clark chin. Right there for all the world to see.

The one that wasn't on *her* face and never had been.

It had made her feel a little dizzy.

It made her curl up in a ball and fight to breathe evenly again.

And for a while there, she hadn't been sure she could. She felt as if she was cracking wide-open, falling to pieces, there on an ostentatious plane flying her off into a future she couldn't begin to imagine.

Delaney hadn't had to imagine her future, ever. She'd always known what it would hold.

The seasons would change. There would be good years and bad. Drought and blight. There were a thousand things that could disrupt the yield, including bankers. But she knew where she'd be.

Her vegetables would grow without her now, and for some reason that was the part that made her throat tight and her eyes burn. She'd stayed where she was, curled up in a ball fighting hard to keep the tears inside, for longer than she thought she should have.

When she got herself back under control, she'd stopped thinking about her garden and had returned to piecing together the life Cayetano seemed to think she'd be stepping into. She hadn't come that close to crying again, but she had found herself...panicky at the notion that *she* might be expected to do the things a princess did. That Cayetano might expect her to do those things.

And more panicky still when she imagined how she would go about telling him she would be doing none of them. That she was here for the adventure, nothing more.

But that wasn't why her heart skipped a beat or two in her chest now. It was because, down below her, she could see the sea.

An actual *sea*.

The first she'd ever seen outside of a television screen.

Delaney could see the waves, topped with the occasional bit of white here and there. She knew it was a part of the greater Mediterranean, and even their likely location on a map. But what caught at her was the color. She'd always known that oceans were meant to be blue, but she'd had no idea what that meant. Not really.

Nothing she'd read had prepared her for all the layers of that blue. Aquamarines and blues and deeper navies, rivaling the sky above.

Needless to say, there was no sea of any kind in Kansas.

She wasn't sure there was even any blue, comparatively speaking. Not on this scale.

And then the plane was flying in over an island that looked like make-believe to Delaney. It was too perfect. Too pretty. She saw those white sand beaches that looked too pristine to touch and then built up into the hillsides, gleaming small communities in whites and more blues and deep terra-cottas. But the plane kept going, circling around until it began a breathtaking descent into a high, green valley. She saw fields, though none of them like the ones she'd left behind. Still, the presence of crops—even if it wasn't corn—made her feel less…adrift, maybe.

Though she suspected she wasn't going to feel like herself for some time.

Because she quite literally *wasn't* herself, and she didn't have the slightest idea how she was meant to deal with that truth.

Her breath seemed to tangle in her throat then, but she swallowed hard. And maybe concentrated that much more fiercely on the fields and villages below her.

She refused to cry again. She was filled with horror at the very idea of *showing* someone else—especially burnt gold and ferocious Cayetano—her emotions. And she couldn't help feeling something more than the mess of loss and uncertainty. It was another hint of that same excitement, and it made her feel worse.

Surely she shouldn't like a single moment of this charade.

Delaney hated herself that she did.

She forced herself to concentrate as the plane descended even further.

And she didn't need to ask. She understood without being told that the fortress she could see on one end of the valley, built into the side of the mountains, was where Cayetano was taking her. The castle he'd mentioned.

Because where else would Cayetano Arcieri, the warlord of the north, rest his head? Of course it was in a forbidding stone citadel with the rest of his world at his feet.

Delaney's reading, all the way across the Atlantic, meant she knew more about him now, too.

Some factions online referred to him the way he'd referred to himself, as warlord.

But others called him the rightful King of Ile d'Montagne.

Delaney didn't know what to call him as they disembarked, particularly as she recognized—without him having to say a word to her in explanation or defense—that he was immediately different here. It wasn't so much that he held himself differently, or even acted differently, it was more that he made sense. The exquisite suit seemed to match the ancient stones, somehow.

As if they both grew bigger, brighter, when connected.

As if they were made of the same material.

She had to fight back a shudder at that.

And another wave of grief at what she'd lost when he'd come to tear her away from the place where she'd made her own kind of sense.

Out on the tarmac, the men who had escorted him in Kansas were joined by even more men, all cut from the same solemn, dangerous cloth. They all spoke the same language that she did not share, but lest she think no one was paying attention to her and make a break for it, Cayetano himself herded her toward another waiting vehicle.

Just as glossy and impressive as the SUVs back home.

She braced herself for another one of his deceptively mild interrogations as the car set off, but he only cast an opaque glance her way— leaving marks behind, she was fairly sure— before taking to his phone again. And though she still couldn't understand a word of what he said, she was certain she recognized that tone.

Commanding. Powerful.

Delaney thought again of the long, in-depth article she'd read on the plane that talked so lyrically about the true King of Ile d'Montagne. The true heir to its long-contested throne.

It turned out that the man who had turned up in the middle of her cornfield was something of a pet cause around the world. The plight of the Ile d'Montagne rebels was discussed in papers and symposiums across the globe. While the peace of some seventy years was lauded, most of the articles suggested it was destined for a bitter, bloody end. Delaney had thought she might ask him about his celebrity—and not his plans for possible bloodshed, as that seemed impolite at best—but she bit the urge back. Because somehow, she doubted very much that his international stature was accidental. She might not know anything about would-be kings or contested land or conflicts stretching back into the Dark Ages, but she knew, with a deep certainty, that Cayetano was exactly the person the articles had made him out to be.

Canny. Deliberate. And more sympathetic. Persuasive in ways his ancestors had not been.

He was, all the articles claimed in one way or another, the greatest threat to the Ile d'Montagne royal family since the last civil war that had killed so many in the late eighteen-hundreds.

And Delaney felt certain, as her heart kicked at her and the blood in her body seemed to heat whenever he was near, that he posed no lesser threat to her.

It was another thing that should have upset her, when instead it made a different kind of anticipation drum through her. Like her blood flowed to a beat.

Instead of concentrating too closely on what that must mean, she looked out the window at the lush green all around, fields and vineyards in the spring sunshine. And at the pretty villages, clustered here and there and certainly not hidden, as they moved ever closer to that fortress carved into the mountain.

It took her some time to realize that Cayetano was no longer on his cell phone.

She snuck a look at him and found him regarding her with that burnt gold consideration that made her shiver. The goose bumps seemed to take on a life of their own, marching down her arms and her spine with a certain resoluteness that made her...breathless.

Just a little bit breathless. Just breathless enough to notice it—and notice him.

Because when he looked at her it was as if she fell forward when she knew she stayed still, toppling out of her seat and catapulting deep into all that gold and heat—

"How do you find my home?" Cayetano asked, in a tone that suggested there was only one answer.

Luckily enough, it was also the only answer she wanted to give.

"It's beautiful." Delaney sat back in her seat, gripping her hands together in her lap and hoping it looked as if maybe she was being whatever *ladylike* was. Not her wheelhouse. "But surely, if you are forever at war yet live out in the open, it would be easy enough to simply come to this valley and get rid of you all."

The gold in his gaze warmed several degrees and she did, too, as if they were connected as surely as he was to this place.

"How bloodthirsty you are," he murmured.

But as if he liked that about her.

It was…disconcerting. It made the beat inside her brighter, somehow. Faster and hotter. "Not at all. I just got the impression that rebel armies usually spend their time hiding in underground tunnels or something."

That impression did not come from any of the articles she'd read today. She was fairly certain it came from the action movies she and Catherine had watched together over the years. But Delaney found she really didn't want to think about things like that. It sat too uneasily in her belly, like the memories themselves were fragile.

Like he could take them from her, too.

Cayetano shifted in his seat to look at her more squarely and that was better, in a way. She felt less fragile. But everything else was… *more*.

"It is no longer the Dark Ages, Delaney." She almost thought he smiled, and a prickle of heat moved over her, washing its way down from her temples to her toes. "We are no longer required to hide ourselves away and pray for deliverance, especially not when a peace has been declared and held for so many years. And, of course, there are no longer pockets of this world where atrocities can be committed without consequences. The internet is everywhere."

Delaney tried not to look as dubious as she felt. "I'm not sure I'd trust my safety to the internet, of all things."

"It is the internet, yes," he agreed after a moment. "For good or ill. But part of why these eyes upon us work is Queen Esme's vanity, far greater than her father's before her, hard as that is to imagine. She wishes to be known as a good queen, you see. I believe Britain's Elizabeth has left an indelible mark on her peers. How can they achieve her longevity or be even a fraction so beloved? Yet Esme has aspirations, almost all of them European. She would find the price too high were she to let her temper take hold."

"I suppose that's something." And better than nothing.

"It is what we tell ourselves, in any case." Again that ghost of a smile. "And as yet, we are still here."

They reached the base of the great fortress and Delaney expected that they would have to get out, and clamber up into it, somehow. She couldn't decide if she welcomed a climb or feared it. But instead, the road led straight into the mountainside.

And when the car did not stop, did not so much as brake, she braced herself—

Only to let her breath out in a rush when she realized that the shadow before her was not shadow at all, but a tunnel.

"It is an optical illusion that has served us well," Cayetano said from behind her, as the interior of the car was cast into the dark of the tunnel. "It is less effective on automobiles than horses, I grant you. But we make it work all the same."

Before Delaney could think of something to say in response to that, the car was barreling back out into the light. And it took her much longer than it should have to realize that they were now in an internal courtyard.

Not a tiny little courtyard, like the ones she'd seen in picture books about castles and keeps. This courtyard was much bigger. Surrounded on all sides by tiers of stone, some with windows cut into the rock, others with open galleries, the whole thing climbing up toward the sun far above.

She was sure there was some militaristic reason for the different levels. She was sure it was all about armies and wars, as her research told her so many castle-ish places were in this part of the world.

But that didn't mean it wasn't beautiful. That

didn't keep the Mediterranean sunshine from cascading down, highlighting the fountains, the greenery, the thick vines dotted with joyful flowers in an astonishing array of colors.

The car finally stopped in front of the grandest of the many entrances around the courtyard, and once again Cayetano was there to usher her from the vehicle. He did not pause to look around or make speeches or whatever it was warlords usually did when returning home. Instead, he swiftly led her inside. She had the impression of graceful archways and cool floors, light-filled rooms and walls filled with the kind of art that only rich people seemed to have. Not something pretty that a person might like to look at every day, like Grandma Mabel's sampler, but dark, dreary paintings of off-putting scenes that no one would ever want to look at too closely or for too long.

That probably means each one is worth its own fortune, she told herself.

Though from her reading, Cayetano didn't need any extra fortunes to go along with his.

It was all dizzying, really. The space. The stone. The obvious grandeur at every turn. She walked and walked, trying to get her bearings, though it proved impossible. Every hallway looked like the one before. And more distracting, Cayetano guided her along with his hand in the small of her back.

It felt like a hot coal, melting off her skin and making her whole body hum.

Making it hard to concentrate on castles and art and directions.

She felt a bit shocked when he took that intense heat away, and was taken back to find herself in a happy little room a few levels up. An elegant sitting room, by the look of it, with more of that sunshine pouring in.

Delaney had seen *Downton Abbey*. She recognized the sort of small couches and meticulously placed tables that she associated with fussy places and the people who inhabited them.

"I must attend to some matters," Cayetano told her, and she understood, then, that he'd been playing a role in Kansas. That the man she'd met there had been accessible in comparison. She caught her breath, even as everywhere else, she burned.

His gaze swept over her as if he knew every flicker, every flame. He ignited her anew, and then he was gone.

Leaving her to run a hand around to the small of her back to see if she could feel the scorch marks he must have left behind.

But the door swung back open almost at

once, and she found herself surrounded by a group of chattering women who exclaimed over her, pantomimed things with their hands that made no sense, and then disappeared again. Though unlike Cayetano, who she suspected could always find matters to claim his attention and no doubt too many of them, she did get the impression that the women would return.

Delaney took the opportunity to take stock of her surroundings in what little time she had to herself. She was standing in the center of a cheerful room, as bright as all the ones they'd passed, which made no sense to her. Weren't they packed in beneath thick walls of stone?

Something about the stones stuck with her, though when she pivoted around in a circle there was nothing offensive anywhere. The paintings were lovely landscapes. The room was done in pale yellows and sweet blues. The walls were stone, yes, and so even though it was not cold outside, Delaney was grateful for the thick rug beneath her feet. She had the feeling it would be much colder in here without it. There were various chairs and fancy little couches and end tables scattered about, all of them loosely grouped in the direction of a big fireplace that looked far too clean to have ever been used.

Was she supposed to sit down? Was this a cell of some kind? Should she go over and test the door to see if she was locked in? Or perhaps gauge if she might need to climb out a window?

Not that she felt as moved toward her escape as she should. She pressed a hand against her heart, but she already knew it was still drumming along, telling her truths she would have much preferred to ignore.

She was still debating what she should do when the door flew open again. Another group of servants streamed in, this time bearing platters of food and a rolling trolley.

And behind them came Cayetano.

Suddenly, it was as if that fire between them was lit in the grate. The room was too hot. Too close. She worried she was suffocating.

Delaney was still where he'd left her, there in the center of the room. And she discovered, as his gaze punched into her, that she was unable to move. She watched, in a kind of panic, as the servants laid out all the dishes they'd brought with them on the largest of the small tables, and then, one by one, disappeared back out into the hall.

Leaving her alone with this man.

She knew her reaction didn't make sense. She'd been alone with him now for hours and hours. She'd willingly gotten into that car in Kansas. She'd boarded that plane. She'd let him carry her off to this fortress and had walked into the stone enclosure on her own two feet. She'd assessed potential escape routes in theory, though she hadn't tried any out.

Yet it only occurred to her now to question what on earth she was *doing*.

"You look like a terrified rabbit," Cayetano informed her, standing some distance away.

Looking almost idle.

A kind of alarm began to beat in her then, for this man was many things, but she was certain that *idle* wasn't one of them.

"Thank you," she squeaked out. She cleared her throat, furious with herself for betraying her internal struggle. "That's not at all condescending."

"It is an accurate description, nothing more."

"What do you intend to do with me?" Delaney demanded, the way she should have before. Long before they landed. Maybe before she'd gotten in his car. "Is this supposed to be a cell? Am I to be locked up here until you wear me down and I agree to marry you just so I can get a glimpse of the sky?"

She got considerably more melodramatic as she spoke, which was shocking, given how little she'd ever given herself over to melodrama before. But all he did was lift one of his dark brows and she forgot to be embarrassed. This wasn't the Midwest. And extraordinary circumstances required unusual responses.

"Surely you have seen the row of windows behind you." She had, of course. She could feel the warm caress of the sunlight even now. Clearly she would have to work on her melodrama if she wanted it to be effective. Assuming *effectiveness* was ever the point of it. "You need only step out on your balcony and look up, Delaney. The sky is where it always is."

"I think that qualifies as avoiding the question," she said primly.

"Why didn't I think of a cell?" he mused, as if to himself. "I believe the castle we stand in is possessed of a dungeon, now that you mention it. I'm sure something could be arranged."

Delaney stood a little straighter. "So you do intend to lock me up until I do what you want?"

He thrust his hands into his pockets, which somehow made the suit he wore look better. Less perfect, yet more rampantly masculine. And it made him look more idle and more dangerous, all at once.

Surely that shouldn't have been possible.

But she was more concerned with how nonchalant his expression was. "Allow me to assure you, little one, that it is unnecessary for me to lock anyone up."

"Let *me* assure *you* that whatever you think

that means, it's not exactly comforting on this end," she shot back at him. "It's also not a *no.*"

"Delaney. Please." He did something with his chin that somehow swept over the small feast laid out on the long, low table between them. "I thought you might be hungry."

"Why would you think that?" she demanded, as if he'd mounted an attack.

"Because I am hungry." His mouth stayed in that straight line, but still, she had the unshakable conviction that he was laughing. Just somewhere she couldn't see. "A not uncommon occurrence after I travel."

She swallowed, hard, not understanding why she felt so…fragile. Though that wasn't quite the right word.

Upended, maybe. Caught out.

But she didn't know what to do about any of the things she felt, so she went and sat on one side of the table in a stuffy sort of chair that made her question her posture. She ignored her sudden debutante concerns and tried to focus instead on the many small plates laid out before her, all laden with things she had never seen on a table in Kansas, yet all smelled and looked wonderful.

Yet the only thing she was really aware of was Cayetano. What he was doing. Or not doing. When he chose to move. When he settled himself opposite her, clearly not concerned that the furniture might be judging him. How he sat and how he looked at her and even what plate he appeared to be eyeing—

That was how she felt, she realized then. Uncomfortably *aware*. Of everything.

Including that spot in the small of her back where he'd touched her, that pulsed like its own flame.

The table was laden with more than enough food for the two of them. There were sweets and cakes on one end. Trays of vegetables, raw and cooked alike and smelling of new and different spices, took up real estate in the middle. And on the other end were cold and roasted meats that smelled so good her belly rumbled. There were what looked like baked casseroles, but with ingredients she could not begin to identify. And the longer she stared, the more she accepted that she didn't have to know what it all was to find it tempting.

And more, that she really was hungry.

She opted not to think about why it slid around inside her like a new heat that Cayetano, a stranger to her in all the ways that mattered, had known that when she hadn't known herself.

Delaney picked up a plate and then set herself to the important task of tasting everything. She barely glanced at Cayetano while she helped herself, then commenced the tasting. It wouldn't help her any to get mixed up in all that dark glory while she was eating, and anyway, she was too busy filling her belly.

When she was deliciously, extravagantly full, she sat back to find him watching her.

Maybe, she admitted to herself, she'd known full well that he'd had his eyes on her all along.

"I imagine those aren't good enough manners," she said when he seemed content to do nothing more than study her. The way he had since he'd stepped out of his car, now that she considered it. "For either the real or fake royal households on this island."

Again, the sense of a smile when there was none. "I see you've been doing your reading."

She was full, pleasantly so, and that made her feel...expansive. Delaney settled back in her own seat and regarded him, for a change. And took her time about it as she studied him. Unapologetically.

This isn't the time to get lost in how starkly beautiful he is, she cautioned herself when her contemplation of his sensual mouth threatened to overtake her.

"I read quite a few articles," she said when she thought she could speak without the fire inside her taking over. "All about Cayetano Arcieri, beloved by celebrities and charities and protesters the world over. They all take turns gushing about your contributions to this island and to the planet. In various interviews."

"The plight of my people moves many," he replied. Easily enough.

"They made it sound as if you fought a war or two to get your position. That's not exactly true, is it?"

His gaze gleamed and she found herself repressing a shiver. "It is not untrue."

"The Arcieris have been a particular thorn in the side of the royals for as long as anyone can remember." She wanted to say that it reminded her of the longstanding feud back where she came from, between Jean Lynnette Baker and Lurleen Snyder about the origin of a potato salad recipe, but thought better of it. She regarded this intense man before her instead. "Haven't you?"

"It is the duty and privilege of the name."

"And all because, a million years ago, there were twins."

He nodded, and now she was sure that there was a definite curve to his mouth. But she had the strangest notion that it was a kind of pride. In her. "Identical brothers. So identical that when the younger twin stepped in and took his older brother's place at the coronation, no one recognized the switch."

"The royal family swears this never occurred."

Cayetano only shrugged. "They would."

"There was a war, led by the twin who claimed the throne."

"The false king." Cayetano shook his head. "Because he believed that if he went on the offense immediately, he could end the argument. By killing anyone who dared stand against him. As tyrants do so like to do."

"The other side was formed by the supposedly deposed twin, who began calling himself one of the family names. Arcieri."

"Indeed."

"So really, give or take a few centuries, you and I are related," Delaney pointed out.

Helpfully.

She thought she saw the flash of his teeth. The gleam in his gaze was brighter, that was a certainty. "If that is how you wish to think of it."

"Well," she said, and managed to make herself sound regretful. "We certainly can't marry if we're related, can we?"

He actually did laugh then, a bark of a sound that made her breath ache a bit. It was so *male*. "It would take a lot more than a tiny drop of shared blood, generations behind us now, to put me off marrying you, Delaney."

"I really think—" she began.

"But no matter how much I might wish to marry you, I won't," he told her, smoothly. "Not at this moment."

That should have been music to Delaney's ears.

Instead, she found herself scowling at him. She did not choose to ask herself why. "Why not?"

If that amused him, too, he didn't show it. Instead, he leaned back in his seat, cocked his head to one side, and merely gazed at her. Then, making sure she was aware he was doing it, he took his time looking her up and down.

And despite herself, Delaney found herself sitting up straighter. Her hands moved to her lap, as if to brush off crumbs she knew weren't there on her favorite pair of jeans. Because she was suddenly much too aware that she was in this make-believe realm of princes and princesses, royal houses and one true kings. And more, she was supposed to belong here by blood.

Maybe, just maybe, her beloved T-shirt that read "MIDWEST IS BEST" was not the appropriate thing to be wearing here.

Cayetano aimed all that burnt gold at her, and

looked, if anything, almost sorrowful. Pitying, even, and no one liked to be *pitied.*

So, really, there was no reason at all that look should make her feel lit up, from the inside out.

"Because I am the true King of Ile d'Montagne," he told her, in that way he had. As if, were she to look closely, she might find these words stamped into her bones. "That is why not. And you are the true heir to the current throne. And the future Queen of this island might very well be the farm girl you call yourself, Delaney. I like that this is how you see yourself. I like the look of your Kansas all over you."

What she felt all over her then was him. That look he was giving her. The fire inside her, crackling higher all the time.

As if she'd never heard of Kansas.

"But no matter how much I might like my farm girl as she is," he said in that same stamped-into-bone way that made her want to sigh and blush and whisper things like *your farm girl.* "I am afraid that here, on this island where you will soon be hailed as the Crown Princess in front of the world, you cannot *look* like one."

CHAPTER SIX

SHE LOOKED SO affronted that Cayetano rather thought she might snatch up one of the small plates and throw it at him. Or a great many of the small plates.

He could admit that no small part of him wished that she would. Because an explosion on that level would require an appropriate response from him.

And he would love nothing more than to… respond.

At length.

The hunger in him felt like a fever. Like a calling. He had no idea how he would hold himself back if she burst into a flame of temper before him.

But all Delaney did was glare at him.

"That is very rude," she admonished him, and to his astonishment he found himself feeling…ever so slightly abashed. Or he assumed that was what the unfamiliar sensation was.

"I did not come to you, claiming a throne or whatever it is people do in situations like this. You're the one who appeared in the middle of my life. And ruined it. If you don't like how I look, well. That sounds a lot to me like a *you* problem."

And he liked the way she looked at him as she said that. As if she were prepared to launch herself over the table to make her point and was only *just* holding herself back.

Just as he was.

Perhaps for the very same reason.

"But you are in my valley now," he replied, leaning back as if he was perfectly at his ease. He should have been. He had been navigating far more treacherous waters than this for the whole of his life. Why should a girl who didn't know who she really was get beneath his skin? "My problems are your problems, you will find. My problems are everyone's problems."

"You are not *my* warlord, Cayetano."

And she made an emphatic little noise when she said that, like punctuation.

He should not have found that charming. If it had been anyone else, he knew he would not have. He would have been far more focused on the disrespect. "I think you will find, little one, that soon enough I will be your everything."

She didn't like that. She sat straighter and she glared at him—but then again, her cheeks warmed.

"That is delusional." She even pointed a finger at him, and it took him a moment to recognize that she was *admonishing* him. "I came here because this is an adventure for me, whatever it might be for you. And I decided it might make sense to meet the people I'm actually related to."

"Yet you have not so much as asked after them."

"I'm hardly going to ask *you* about them." Her chin rose. "You are their sworn enemy, by all accounts, including yours."

"I had no idea genealogy intrigued you so." He fought to keep the smile from his face and did not think too hard about how unusual an occurrence it was that he should wish to smile at all. "You seemed uninterested in it back in Kansas. Your blood was of no matter to you. I am sure you said as much."

"People who can trace their ancestors back several centuries shouldn't comment on those of us who learned we were an entirely different person only days ago," Delaney retorted. "Of course I want to meet my…the woman who actually gave birth to me. Eventually."

He did not miss the way she looked away

when she said that. As if she was in no rush to meet Queen Esme, and not for the usual reasons. He suspected that if she thought too much about the Queen, this might become real to her.

Clearly, she didn't want that.

"I was under the impression you came here because your mother told you to," he said. "No more and no less."

"Thanks to you, I now have to grapple with the fact that—biologically speaking—she's not my mother."

And she said that tartly enough, but there was something about the way she held herself that made him regret… Well, he couldn't regret what he had done. He could never regret something that would shortly put him on the path to finally right such an ancient wrong. But he regretted, more than he would have thought possible before this very moment, that finding her and telling her who she was had hurt her.

It changed nothing.

But still, he felt it.

And he did not like such things. *Feelings.* He had been avoiding them for most of his life. Feeling anything at all made him certain he was on a collision course with the fate that had met his parents. Death. Dishonor.

He refused.

"I think you're laboring under a misconception," he said, in a more repressive tone than he might have used had she not inspired him to *emote*. "I did not ask you for your hand in marriage and then wait, filled with a trembling hope, for your answer. I informed you that our wedding would take place. I imagine you think that a display of arrogance."

"Extreme arrogance," Delaney agreed too swiftly, color high. "Appalling, rude, delusional arrogance."

"Little one, that is merely me," Cayetano replied, and lifted an unconcerned shoulder. "What you should concern yourself with are the ancient laws of this island, in which I very much doubt you are conversant no matter how many internet articles you read."

She had gaped a bit at the *that is merely me* bit. Now she snapped her mouth shut and glared at him. "Let me guess. You can lock a girl in a tower and everyone shrugs and says, *Oh, well, I guess you get to keep her.* Like women are nothing more than fireflies you can collect in a jar."

Cayetano could not remember the last time he had stopped to appreciate the fireflies that heralded the summers here. When as a small child, he had delighted in them. He could re-call running, barefoot, through the fields while his parents walked behind, trying to catch the little bursts of light that popped in the air all around them—

The memory fell like ice water through him, horrifying him. He was not a man given to nostalgia. It smacked of those emotions he abhorred.

"This is not a jar," he replied with what he thought was admirable patience. "It is Arcieri Castle, built with painstaking care across the ages. First hidden, its residents and servants risking death if they were discovered here. Sometimes its own kind of cell, because my ancestors weathered many a siege within these walls. Now open to celebrate the peace. But never a mere jar."

Naturally, his farm girl did not look impressed by anything he said. He had never encountered another human so devoutly unimpressed, in fact. She sat there on a priceless settee in jeans and a T-shirt, in an ancient castle renowned for its beauty, and dared to glare at him as if he was the offending party here.

"None of that makes it any less of a cell," she told him, in a tone he could only call *mulish.* "Whether it was built in two days or two millennia, and no matter what it means to you and your people, it amounts to the same thing."

Cayetano sighed. "There is no need for cells.

Still, as I said, there are old ways. This is a very old place."

"I may be American, but I'm capable of understanding dates. And history."

He found her tone excessively dry. But once again, the problem with his lost princess was that he found himself fascinated by her total lack of awe in his presence. He had seen a hint of it in that dusty yard in Kansas, but it had faded. Quickly.

It was the novelty, nothing more, he told himself. Any moment now, he would stop thinking about her as a woman, as an individual, as *his*. And get back to thinking about her role here and how best to deploy her upon the unsuspecting House of Montaigne.

Before he'd gone to Kansas, that deployment had been his fondest fantasy.

"Some of our old ways are enshrined in law as well as custom," he told her, maintaining his posture of seeming ease when he did not feel easy. He was not making up the old ways here. He could marry her in the morning if he chose, ending this farce that she had a choice in the matter that quickly. Cayetano liked that notion. A lot.

But it did not strike him as particularly strategic. He reminded himself that he had already won—she was here. What would it hurt to attempt to woo her a little?

Or, at the very least, not rush her.

"Let me guess," Delaney said in the same dry way. "The men in charge forgot to update things around here because why bother? They like it medieval."

Cayetano ran his tongue around his teeth and abandoned any *wooing* plans. "It is not necessary to imprison you, Delaney. I need only keep you for a night, then claim you in front of my brethren come the dawn. Only one, if I like, though at least three is more traditional."

She stared at him as if waiting for more, then scowled when no more was forthcoming. "That's barbaric."

"It was necessary in a certain era." Cayetano waved an idle hand. Mostly to infuriate her. A success, if the look in her blue eyes was any indication. And he should not have taken such pleasure in these games. This woman was a means to an end, not a pleasure. He could not fathom why he kept forgetting that. Or why, despite himself, the way he wanted her felt more like a roar within him every moment. "There was a time when this island was far more lawless than it is now. Times were perilous and lives were short. Men in need of wives took them where they could, and it became necessary to make sure that their children were legitimate."

"You can't *take* me," she said. And it took tremendous control on his part to refrain from pointing out that he had already done just that. That she had packed for the privilege. "I demand that you release me."

"Little one," Cayetano said, his voice rich with amusement, "where do you think you are? This is not the American Embassy. The only person who can intercede on your behalf with me...is me."

Her breath left her in an audible rush. Her mouth opened and shut more than once, before her cheeks flushed red and she snapped her teeth closed. It took her a fair few moments to gather herself once more.

"You cannot think that this will actually work," she seethed at him.

He found himself caught, anew, at her reaction. There was no hint of fear on her face, which would have stopped him at once. Or made him approach this differently, at any rate. But she didn't look remotely uncomfortable. If anything, she was ablaze.

At the *injustice,* unless he missed his guess.

And Cayetano was very rarely wrong when it came to reading people.

Though he was finding it difficult to read

himself tonight. Why should her reaction, whatever it might be, make his body tighten with desire? He was not used to this intensity. Not for anything but his purpose, his promises.

He hated the very idea that a person could turn him from his lifelong path. Was he no better than his parents after all?

The very notion appalled him.

"I do not wish it to work," he told her, more severely than was necessary. Perhaps he was directing that at himself. "I would far prefer that you decide, of your own volition, to marry me. Freely. Who would not wish this? I do not want a prisoner for bride, Delaney. But you should know this about me now. I will always do what I must. When it comes to this island, and my people, I always will."

She seemed almost electrified, as if a current ran through her. She shook slightly—but with temper, he thought, still not fear. Then, suddenly, she shot to her feet, her hands in fists at her side that suggested that he was right. "None of this is okay."

He might not understand himself this day, but he did like to be right.

"I do not think this the tragedy you're making out to be," he countered, and it was easy, in the face of her outrage, to sound very nearly lazy again. "Please bear in mind that in order to achieve my goals, I am forced into the match as much as you. There are worse things than wedding a stranger, Delaney. Trust me on this."

Her blue eyes were a storm. "That's easy for you to say. You're the one doing this."

"Because I must," he said again. With finality.

"But *why*?" she threw at him, as if the query was torn from somewhere deep inside her.

He would not have responded to temper. He would have laughed at a demand. But he found he couldn't ignore a plea like this, as if it hurt her.

"This is a fractured place," he told her, and this was no prepared speech. The words simply welled up from within him. "It has been broken for so long that the people here have come to imagine that they are broken, too. And nothing will fix it. No talks. No treaties. No wars. As long as there are two sides, there will be conflict. It is my job—my calling—to do what I can to dispel it. Not because I do not have the same urges as the rest of my people, to rise up and take what was taken from us. Of course I do. But I know that in these skirmishes, we all lose. I am so tired of loss, Delaney."

He had never said such a thing out loud before. He had not known the words existed within him.

He wasn't at all sure that he liked knowing that they'd been there all along, but he pushed on. "But there is only one way we can do away with these sides. Not so that I can win a throne, but so all of us can win back what was taken from us so long ago. So that we can move forward without this loss that marks all of us, royalist and rebel alike. We can only be whole if we come together."

She stared at him, round-eyed. "You truly believe this."

"I do."

And he had made a great many vows in his life. To himself. To his people.

This was not a vow, but it felt like one. Like bright, hot steel pressed into flesh.

He could feel it in his skin. Directly over his heart, a terrible, marvelous brand of truth.

Cayetano hardly knew what to do with the storm in him then. Instead, he watched as she blew out a breath, punched those fists of hers into place on her hips, and began to pace around the room.

"I don't understand this…sitting around in pretty rooms and *talking*," Delaney seethed at him, her blue eyes shooting sparks when they met his. "I like to be outside. I like dirt under my feet. I like a day that ends with me having to scrub soil out from beneath my fingernails."

She glared at the walls as if they had betrayed her.

Then at him, as if he was doing so even now.

For a moment he almost felt as if he had—but that was ridiculous.

"When you are recognized as the true Crown Princess of Ile d'Montagne, the whole island will be your garden," he told her. Trying to soothe her. He wanted to lift a hand to his own chest and massage the brand that wasn't there, but *soothing* was for others, not him. He ignored the too-hot sensation. "You can work in the dirt of your ancestors to your heart's content."

Delaney shot a look at him, pure blue fire. "Even if I did agree to do such a crazy thing, you still wouldn't get what you want. It doesn't matter what blood is in my veins. I am a farm girl, born and bred. I will never look the part of the Princess you imagine. Never."

She sounded almost as final as he had, but Cayetano allowed himself a smile, because that wasn't a flat refusal. It sounded more like a *maybe* to him.

He could work with *maybe*.

In point of fact, he couldn't wait.

He rose then. And he made his way toward her, watching the way her eyes widened. The way her lips parted. There was an unmistakable flush on her cheeks as he drew near, and he could see her pulse beat at her neck.

Cayetano was the warlord of these mountains and would soon enough be the King of this island. And he had been prepared to ignore the fire in him, the fever. The ways he wanted her that had intruded into his work, his sleep. But here and now, he granted himself permission to want this woman. *His* woman. Because he could see that she wanted him.

With that and her *maybe,* he knew he'd already won.

"Let me worry about how you look," he said as he came to a stop before her, enjoying the way she had to look up to hold his gaze. It made her seem softer. He could see the hectic need all over her, matching his own. "There is something far more interesting for you to concentrate on."

Delaney made a noise of frustration. "The barbaric nature of ancient laws and customs?"

"Or this."

And then Cayetano followed the urge that had been with him since he'd seen her standing in a dirt-filled yard with a battered kerchief on her head and kissed her.

He expected her to be sweet. He expected to enjoy himself.

He expected to want her all the more, to

tempt his own feverish need with a little taste of her.

But he was totally unprepared for the punch of it. Of a simple kiss—a kiss to show her there was more here than righting old wrongs and reclaiming lost thrones. A kiss to share a little bit of the fire that had been burning in him since he'd first laid eyes on her.

It was a blaze and it took him over.

It was a dark, drugging heat.

It was a mad blaze of passion.

It was a delirium—and he wanted more.

He drew her closer to him, then hauled her up into his arms, letting the fever take hold of him, a delicious madness. He kissed her again, then again. Delaney made a low, broken sort of sound and he made as if to retreat, but she threw her arms around his neck and held on.

And then there was nothing at all but the pounding of his heart, and the hard pulse of need in his sex. The slick fire with every angle, every dance of his tongue and hers.

The glory of it. The desire.

He found his hands moving over her, wild with need. As if they moved of their own accord, and ached to glance over each and every part of her—

My God, you're losing control—

That voice inside him shocked him into stillness.

Cayetano set her aside abruptly, his breath hard and raw.

And almost lost control of himself again when he saw that her blue eyes were two shades darker. While her pretty mouth was faintly swollen from his.

Not reaching out for her again felt like a blow.

"Is that reason enough?" he managed to grit out. "Do you think that happens every day?"

Delaney blinked at that, then swallowed hard. She looked vulnerable for a moment, and that clawed at him, but then she straightened her shoulders and lifted that stubborn chin. "Speak for yourself. It happens three times a day for me. Sometimes more."

He moved away from her, because it was that or continue as he had been and take her right there against the wall, and he couldn't allow that. He needed to figure out how it was he had lost his composure here. He had to make sure that he was in control of himself the way he always, always was.

Because this flirtation with chaos could never happen again.

"You have two choices," he told her when he could speak without shouting—another red flag—and he was aware that his voice had gone arctic. There was no helping it. Everything inside him was on fire, but God only knew what would become of him if he showed her that. If he allowed himself such a display. The very idea chilled him to the bone. "You may agree to marry me. If you do this, our wedding will take place in one month. It will give us time to prepare the perfect way to launch you and what you mean upon the House of Montaigne, and the world. Because it must be perfect. Meanwhile, you can study up on your relatives, if you wish. We have a great many books on the topic in our libraries, plus any number of personal experiences. And while you are learning where you come from, we will prepare for where you're going. We'll make you the Queen my country deserves."

"And the second choice?" she asked without missing a beat.

Her eyes were glittering with temper now.

Cayetano inclined his head. "The second choice is simple enough. My men will stand guard outside your door. Come the morning, I will gather my people in the courtyard and claim you as mine as if it is still the Dark Ages. It will be done, and we will spend the same amount of time readying ourselves for our unveiling. But you won't be trusted, and I fear that you might find Arcieri Castle more of a cell than you might otherwise."

"So the choice you're offering me is really no choice at all."

There were too many competing shadows inside him, and he did not have the grip on himself he should. "If I were you, my little farm girl, I would count myself lucky I had any choice at all."

"And do I get two different marriages to choose from, too?" she asked, folding her arms in front of her. As if she had all the self-control he was appalled to discover he lacked.

"I beg your pardon?"

"Does a barbarous beginning lead to brutality?" she demanded. "Is that what I have to look forward to?"

She could not have said anything that would have cut him more.

"I would never lift my hand to a woman," Cayetano bit out, though even as he did, something in him pointed out that if she thought otherwise she surely wouldn't have said such a thing, and so baldly. Maybe that was what spurred on the words that came out of him then, as if the desire in him had taken him over completely. "The only battles you and I will have will be in bed. But both of us will win. And the only question will be how much you can take."

There was something about the stunned sort of way she stared back at him that got to him. That made him think she was not necessarily as sophisticated as she pretended in the midst of her defiance. And that would mean...

But he dismissed it.

And then Cayetano forced himself to leave her in that sitting room before he could think better of it.

Before he could show her what he meant, there and then.

Before he betrayed himself any further.

CHAPTER SEVEN

DELANEY HAD NO choice but to pick the first option. Because she certainly wasn't prepared to find herself barbarically married tomorrow morning.

What else could she do in the wake of that kiss? Of that...hurricane that had swept her away before she knew what was happening to her, making a mockery of any *weather systems* she thought she knew before?

Her body was no longer recognizable to her. She no longer felt like herself, as if he'd taken her from the uncertain ground of learning she wasn't a Clark head-on into the sea she'd seen out the window, shifting and moving and no ground at all beneath her feet. There were too many wild sensations simmering inside her. Too much longing.

As if all that was left of her—the only part of her that was *her*—was that blooming, near-incapacitating ache that suffused her as he left.

What would you have done if he hadn't stopped? she asked herself after he'd gone and she was left to try to find her breath, her own ragged breath loud in the quiet room.

But no matter how many times she asked herself, it was always the same unsatisfactory answer.

Surrender.

Delaney tried to ignore the heavy heat that rushed through her every time she thought that word. Every time she imagined what surrendering to a man like that, stone and fire, might do to her...

What was the matter with her that some part of her craved that kind of immolation? She wanted him to kiss her again. She wanted to lose herself in it, and then find herself there in his arms. She had the half-mad notion that it was only there that she might feel like herself again. Only there she might truly come *alive*. She wanted—

A servant stepped in while she was still standing where Cayetano had left her, clinging to the wall. Delaney was sure he must have been able to see how red she was. How disheveled. How off-balance. Though if he did, no trace of his reaction showed on his face.

"The warlord wishes to know your choice," the man said with great dignity.

Delaney wanted to pretend she didn't know what he meant, but that felt a bit beneath her.

"The first one," she told him, trying to match his dignity with some measure of poise and grace—or at least calm. "Thank you."

It was a month. A lot could happen in a month. He might come to his senses, for one thing. She told herself that was what she wanted. Meanwhile, she would use the library he'd mentioned to educate herself on what she'd walked into here. Not only about her biological family, but about the Arcieris and their castle, too.

She'd hardly had a chance to breathe, much less think. Her new reality had been thrust at her, and now she was in this strange and overwhelming place, and Cayetano had kissed her like one or both of them were dying—

You're all right now, she told herself. *Perfectly alive and well and* yourself. *You can start using your head again.*

Relief flooded her. She pressed her feet into the floor beneath her, assuring herself that she stood on her own two feet, as always. It would cost her nothing to stay here. She could go along with Cayetano as long as it suited her and gather all kinds of information before she was forced to face the Queen who was, apparently, her mother. Or the Princess who had taken her place on this island—yet belonged back home in the Kansas that Delaney loved.

She told herself this was nothing more than a delaying tactic. And more, that she was in control.

Weddings don't necessarily happen overnight, Catherine had said. *No need to rush into anything.*

That was what Delaney was doing. Not rushing.

After Cayetano's man left, she moved away from the wall. She frowned at the feast still laid out on the table, trying to decide if she was actually hungry or just feeling the very real need to eat all her feelings. But before she could get to repressing with pastries, the original trio of female servants swept back in.

They carried her battered old duffel bag with them. They were bright and chattery, like three happy birds, and they didn't appear to require any response from Delaney.

That was a good thing. Delaney was still having more trouble standing on her own two feet than she cared to admit.

"Are you well?" one of the women asked, possibly noticing the way Delaney wobbled.

"Jet lag," Delaney said with great authority for someone who had never been on a jet before today.

But she knew it wasn't *jet lag*.

It was that kiss. It was Cayetano. It was that part of her that thought surrender sounded terrific and why not go ahead and marry the *dark glory* that had come for her like a tornado, lifted her up and out of Kansas like she was Dorothy after all, and brought her here?

Because that's what happens in books, Delaney lectured herself, though her attempt to sound internally stern was a bit stymied by all that delirious sensation she could still feel inside her, lighting her up. *Real life is different.*

Though it was, admittedly, hard to cling to her idea of what reality *ought* to be when she was standing in an actual *castle*.

The trio of servants threw open a pair of doors that Delaney hadn't even known were there. She'd thought they were part of the wall. But it turned out that she was already in a kind of apartment, equipped with everything from her own kitchenette to a vast bedroom that opened up onto its own balcony that overlooked the sweep of the valley.

The bedroom alone, she was pretty sure, was bigger than the farmhouse.

The entire farmhouse. And the bed looked about the size of her vegetable patch.

She felt itchy. The whole thing—the pageant of it, the obvious wealth, the fact that there were *servants* who treated her with a sort of brisk deference—made her deeply uncomfortable.

A lot like she was coming out of her skin, she thought, as she was led on a tour through one beautiful room after the next, all apparently a part of her guest quarters. It was a far cry from the inflatable mattress on a floor that had served as the farm's guest accommodations. All the smug paintings and complacent vases. All the self-aggrandizing rugs, so thick and pristine she very much doubted anyone else had walked across their intricate designs. Even the parade of carefully chosen colors seemed condescending to her. Who would ever choose a mint green? A pale yellow? Then anoint it all with gleaming gold and silver and sanctimonious furnishings?

She longed for the simplicity of her real life. The demands of crops, livestock. The inevitability of the seasons. Rain. Sun. Storms. Drought. Those were the things that mattered, not a castle on a mountain above an island she'd never heard of before. Not all these trappings of a kind of moneyed life she couldn't even begin to understand.

Maybe she didn't want to understand.

One thing she could tell she most certainly did not wish to understand was servants.

She'd never had a servant in her life. Clarks did for themselves or they did without.

"I know I'm not a Clark," she muttered, before she felt compelled to remind herself, and smiled when the servant with her in the bedroom—flinging open curtains and doors and bustling this way and that—looked at her quizzically.

Maybe if she kept saying that, it would start making sense. And maybe if she did it enough, she would believe it.

And maybe you're happy at the notion of hiding away here, researching and reading and distancing yourself in all your not rushing, *because you don't want to face the truth,* came a voice inside her, tart enough to be her grandmother's. *You want to put off reality as long as possible.*

What she wanted, Delaney thought then, was not to collapse on the floor and cry.

Because she was afraid that if she started up again, she might never stop.

Delaney squeezed the bridge of her nose until the heat there dissipated. But then she didn't know what to do with herself. There appeared to be nothing for her *to* do but stand about as the women breezed around her in the overlarge bedchamber, chattering brightly as they unpacked her clothes and set out her few personal things. Her attempt to help was swiftly rebuffed with a laugh, so she...stood there near the gigantic four-poster bed that she worried she'd need a ladder to climb into, feeling awkward.

So awkward that it took her a moment to realize that they were speaking to each other, and sort of *at* her, in English.

"I thought everyone spoke French here," she said.

A tad too bluntly, she realized, when all three women—who she was only now realizing were probably about her own age, a fact she probably shouldn't have found so astonishing—stopped what they were doing and gazed at her.

"French, yes. Also, Italian," one of the women said. "But the world is big and speaks more than two languages. So, also Spanish. German. And, yes, English."

"I have a smattering of Japanese," another woman boasted.

But the third one laughed. "Knowing how to say thank-you in Japanese is not a smattering," she said. "It's one word. *Arigato.*"

Delaney felt as if she ought to apologize for speaking only the one. But didn't.

"Also," the first one said as the other two glared at each other, "the warlord insisted that only English-speaking servants wait on you. It caused quite a commotion."

"I'm not surprised," Delaney said. "I can't imagine who would want to wait on a farm girl from Kansas."

All three women looked confused. They looked at each other, then back at Delaney.

"Everyone wanted to wait on you," the third girl said, as if she didn't understand why Delaney had uttered such blasphemy.

"It's an honor," agreed the second.

"You are to be the warlord's bride," said the first. Rapturously. "What greater honor could there be than to attend you?"

Delaney did not have an answer to that. Her body seemed to respond on its own. She told herself it was shame and horror, that thick current of sensation that coiled low in her belly as the words *the warlord's bride* chased around and around in her head. She told herself her body was staging a revolt at the very idea.

But she knew better.

She remembered that kiss too well, and she knew better.

Still, she didn't have a lot of time alone to sit and brood about it.

Because the three servants moved on from the awkward moment, getting down to business quickly. They unpacked everything from her duffel, and then examined it. Critically. One of them pulled out a tape measure. Another produced a pad and pen and noted down the numbers. And only smiled when Delaney asked why.

After they finished whirlwinding around her, they delivered her to another servant waiting for her outside her guest apartment. He wore a uniform that even Delaney's untutored eye could identify as fancy. Fancier than the women, certainly.

And significantly fancier than Delaney in her jeans and T-shirt.

"I am the majordomo," the man intoned.

Then waited for her to reply to that in a proud manner that suggested a bended knee on her part might not be out of the question.

When Delaney did not alter the position of her knees, or change expression at all, he sniffed. Then proceeded to take her on a tour of the castle, stopping along the way to point out objects of note, paintings of historical figures—most, if not all, of the Arcieris—rooms wherein great moments in Ile d'Montagne's history took place, and, at every window, a detailed description of the view. What lands, buildings, villages were before her, their significance, how they had disguised their true purpose during periods of conflict, and so on.

It took her longer than it should have to realize that this was not a tour. It was a lesson.

She blamed the jet lag again, but once she caught on, she paid much closer attention.

And chose not to ask herself why, when she was obviously not going to stay here, she felt it necessary to learn anything about this place. She told herself she was listening so intently because this was, in its way, a story about her family, too. Who better to tell the story than her family's enemies? After listening to a litany of complaints against the Montaigne family across the ages, she could surely only be pleasantly surprised by Queen Esme one day.

She took in all the commentary about the Montaigne line, filing it all away to look up on her own later. To see how the story changed depending on the telling. But she couldn't help but notice that, somehow, she was also interested not only in the details of the castle they stood in, and the valley she could see on the other side of the windows, but of Cayetano himself.

Knowing the enemy, she told herself stoutly. That's all this was. She was *gathering intelligence,* the way people did when embroiled in games involving castles and queens.

"The Arcieri family have controlled the castle almost without interruption since its inception," the majordomo told her while standing in front of a portrait of a long-ago warlord, clearly taking great personal pride in both the image and the Arcieris. "They have been the heart, soul, and conscience of this island these many ages."

Delaney could see Cayetano in the portrait of his ancestor. Stone and fire. Eyes like a hawk.

She could still feel his hard mouth moving on hers.

"It does make a person question what the royal family actually wants, though, doesn't it?" she asked.

The majordomo looked at her as if he'd never heard such blasphemy. "It is abundantly clear that what the Montaignes want is power."

Delaney nodded at him. "But if this one family—" *my family,* she thought, to try to get used to it "—has been the problem for generations, why didn't they just take out the family instead of all these wars and skirmishes and whatever else?"

The way the man looked at her reminded her that she was standing there in another gleaming room, this one a gallery, with the smell of the farm all over her. In her T-shirt and jeans, which were as comfortable as they had ever been but really didn't match her surroundings. And the way he was looking at her, she was tempted to look and see if, in fact, she was also covered in dirt.

"They have tried, madam," said the man before, frostily. "They have tried and tried."

"It's really amazing, then," Delaney said hurriedly, "that the Arcieris have managed to stand against them all the while."

Them in this case being the bad guys whose blood ran in her veins.

When all she'd ever wanted was Kansas dirt and a long, fruitful growing season.

Her words seemed to mollify her companion, though the look he gave her was still ripe with suspicion. "It was not so long ago that we were certain the great cause was lost," he told her, straightening the resplendent coat of his uniform as if it had somehow become imperfect during this lesson. When it had not. "Our current warlord's parents…" But he stopped himself. "I do not wish to speak out of turn."

Delaney wanted nothing more than for him to speak out of turn. At length.

Because she was buying time and collecting information, she assured herself. That little leap inside at the mention of Cayetano was nothing to worry about. Maybe it was heartburn after whatever she'd eaten earlier. She'd never had heartburn before, ever, but these were extraordinary circumstances. If it persisted, she thought as serenely as she could, she would have to ask for the warlord version of antacids.

"It is only history, surely," she said mildly now, keeping her eyes on the picture of the historical warlord before her. He was very impressive, but not as impressive as the current version. But she was quite sure that if she showed even the slightest bit of prurient interest, the already-not-so-sure-about-her majordomo would go silent altogether.

She must have showed the appropriate amount of respectful disinterest, because he continued. "Our warlord's father died when he was quite young and Cayetano became the hope of our people. But for a time it seemed that hope was to be dashed. His mother ruled our people in Cayetano's stead, for he was underage. Some factions believed that she was Arcieri enough, having been married to the previous warlord, and could lead us where we needed to go. But then she considered remarrying, and things became more complicated." He shook his head. "Her choice of a potential husband was no Arcieri. I will leave it at that."

Delaney snuck a look at his expression then, and found it...troubling.

And she didn't like that at all. Because all the things the majordomo did not say seemed thick in the air then, and it made her feel more sympathetic to Cayetano.

When she had no desire to feel the slightest hint of sympathy for him.

Not when she could feel the aftereffects of that hurricane, still kicking up a fuss inside her.

"That must have been hard for the warlord," she said anyway. From some unknown place inside herself, where she was gentle and not the least bit stormy.

"Our warlord is a great man," the major-domo told her, in unmistakable tones of awe. "What would bring other men to their knees only makes Cayetano stronger."

She was still mulling that over when he delivered back to what he called her *rooms* with Ile d'Montagne history in her head and a strange worry for Cayetano in what she was terribly afraid was her heart, to find the same three servants buzzing around. They were laying out garments and if she wasn't mistaken, that was a curling iron she saw being plugged in.

"Surely it's time to rest," she protested.

Because she had never been so tired. She wanted to *droop*.

This is maybe real jet lag, a voice inside suggested. *Because it's an actual thing, not just an excuse.*

"Don't be silly," one of her servants was saying gaily. "We have to get you ready for dinner."

"The warlord regrets that he is unable to dine

with you this evening," said another, with the kind of giggle that Delaney associated with memories of middle school. As if Cayetano was some kind of boy band singer.

"You will be dining with the Signorina instead," said the third.

"The Signorina?"

Delaney didn't know what to do as they swarmed around her, so she stayed still. She didn't object when they started looking at her clothes as if they meant to remove them right there where she stood in the middle of the bedroom floor. Or even when they did.

She was so exhausted and overwhelmed it didn't seem real.

And they were so matter-of-fact about the whole thing that it felt perfectly acceptable, in this strange, unreal place, to find herself surrendering. They tugged everything off and whisked a silk bathrobe of sorts into place so seamlessly that she had the possibly half-hysterical urge to ask if they had choreographed it. Then they spun her around, making clucking noises as they sat her in front of a mirror in what she hadn't recognized was a vanity table in the separate apartment that was her bathroom. Though calling it a *bathroom* didn't really cover the many rooms, nooks, and walk-in closets that were each bigger than the farm-house's whole attic.

Delaney couldn't really process anything, it turned out. So it seemed reasonable enough—or almost—to let someone work on her hair while the other two kept holding different garments that weren't hers in the mirror's reflection, then conferring.

Why not? something in her asked.

After all, she had a whole month. Surely she could effect her escape later—or rather simply leave without all the melodrama.

Not tonight.

"The Signorina is the foremost expert on manners and customs in the valley," Delaney was informed. The girl applying the hairbrush and curling iron to her hair looked very serious as she said this. "She has dedicated herself to the Arcieri family. She has been the governess not only for the warlord, but for his father before him. It is a great honor that she has agreed to this."

Once again, Delaney was aware that she was being studied. For her reaction.

She made what she hoped were noises that suggested she felt appropriately honored.

After they finished fussing with the hair she usually paid no attention to, or put into braids to really ignore, she was packed into a dress that was finer than any other single garment she'd ever beheld. It was soft. It seemed to *whisper* at her, little secrets about its own finery.

Delaney wanted to hate it on principle. But she couldn't.

When they angled her so she could look at her full reflection, something in her…seized, maybe. Or went so still it amounted to the same thing. The woman looking back at her from the mirror wore a dress that belonged behind glass somewhere, maybe in Hollywood. The rope of pearls wound around her neck felt silky against her skin but looked impossibly elegant—a word that had never been used in reference to a girl who spent most of her life in dirty overalls. Never, ever. And it was all topped off with the kind of sophisticated twisty updo that made her look like a complete stranger.

She understood, then. This was a dream. Or it felt like a dream, and that was why she was simply going along with the whole thing, because that was what a person did in dreams. What did it matter that none of this made sense? It didn't have to.

Because in a dream, it wasn't necessary to check with her feelings of dislocation and despair on the one hand and something too much like desire on the other. It wasn't necessary to untangle that knot. Or face this shocking joy in things she would have said repulsed her, like a pretty dress that moved around her legs like it was made of light. If it was real life, she would have had to square up to all the things that were happening to her and had already happened. In a dream, she might as well decide to give herself over to the sheer madness all around her without complaint. So that was what she did.

And a person who was wide awake might have objected to being marched down to what the majordomo had told her was the private wing of the palace, where she was shown into a dining room. But the dreamer in her simply went along with it.

There were only two places set at one end of a glossy table in this new room, packed to the ceiling with the kinds of priceless artifacts she'd been told so much about today, but what caught her attention wasn't more vases and candelabras. It was the tiny woman with an enormous beehive hairdo who waited, peering at Delaney through a pair of spectacles.

Delaney had the strangest urge to curtsy.

When she wasn't sure she even knew *how* to curtsy.

The doors closed behind her, and then there she was. Shut in yet another room in this castle, this time with a diminutive woman who emanated a certain intensity that made Delaney feel…

Well, unfortunately awake, for one thing. But also as if she didn't quite fit in her skin. As if everything about her was *wrong.*

And she realized with a start that she hated it.

More than hated it.

Because Delaney was used to feeling personally comfortable in her own skin. She was used to feeling grounded. Centered. She knew who she was. She knew what her life held and would always hold.

She'd taken pleasure in those things. She'd enjoyed them.

And now she was standing here in clothes that weren't hers, her hair twisted beyond recognition, while a strange woman eyed her down the length of a strange room as if *she* was somehow the problem.

"I take it that I'm supposed to be intimidated by you," Delaney said.

The tiny woman moved only one eyebrow. It rose up, edging toward her towering beehive that made up the better part of her height. "Are you not?"

Her English sounded precise, but with a hint of an accent. Only the barest hint.

"I'm used to a farm," Delaney told her. "The livestock does get a little fractious and plants are known troublemakers, but you learn to deal with it. But no, I wouldn't say that I'm ever intimidated by posturing."

She expected temper. Or more of that haughty affront she'd seen from the major-domo.

But instead, the older woman cackled.

"Marvelous," she cried, clapping her hands together. "You're wildly inappropriate and borderline offensive, and that's what makes you perfect. This will be fun."

She waved Delaney to the seat at the head of the table, still laughing, and settled into the other seat. "Come," she urged Delaney when she hung back. "Everything must be quite strange to you here, myself included, but the food is phenomenal."

And she waited so expectantly that Delaney found herself moving to sit down. Then, not knowing what to do with herself, she watched as the other woman rang the bell beside her dramatic place setting. Vigorously. The sound was still hanging in the air as servants swept in, laden down with trays of food.

"Tonight, we eat," the Signorina said as Delaney blinked down at the array of utensils and piles of plates heaped before her. "We will concern ourselves with the stuffy rules of etiquette tomorrow."

Delaney was shocked to find that she spent a surprisingly enjoyable evening in the Signorina's company. It wasn't until she was in her absurdly oversize bed, finally alone, that she remembered that she really wasn't supposed to enjoy any part of this.

Why not? a voice inside her asked. Sounding a lot like Catherine, who was merrily not taking Delaney's calls—the way she had the summer Delaney had gone to camp for one miserable week.

"You're supposed to be trying to figure out how to *not* marry that man," she told herself sternly. "Or at the very least, discovering things about the Montaignes. And therefore, you."

But she dropped off to sleep before she could start coming up with a plan to do just that.

And as one day became several days, then a week, Delaney realized two things. One, that she didn't seem to be in any hurry to come up with a plan, and she probably ought to think about why that was. And two, that she knew how Cayetano expected to wait out his month.

He'd put her on a schedule.

Because the days followed a sort of pattern. During the day, there was usually some time dedicated to wardrobe concerns and somehow this led to more and more items in those spacious closets that went on forever. And her three bright and cheerful servants never seemed to be able to find the clothes that Delaney had brought with her, so sorry, so they used the new clothes instead. They dressed her for every meal save breakfast, which she was allowed to eat in her bathrobe while they bustled around her, telling her what her day would hold.

Delaney told herself she hated these things, but the truth was that she quite liked the clothes that were picked out for her. She liked the hair, the makeup, which she would never have done for herself. She was getting more and more comfortable with the stranger in the mirror.

She told herself that it was in her blood, the inner Princess she'd never known was there.

Even though, if she was honest, her blood scared her a little. Maybe more than a little. Not the battles recorded in musty old books. She figured that was history. Packed full of events no one wanted to happen to them—but then, history was a lot closer on this side of the Atlantic. People here spoke of the fourteen-hundreds as if they were last Tuesday. What scared her was that the old books with the gold-edged pages weren't filled with tedious facts she would need to regurgitate for some test.

They were records of things her family did.

Mostly to Cayetano's family.

And she didn't want to feel connected to either part of that equation. She was supposed to be having an adventure, not finding herself in history books. Especially not when what she should have wanted was to find her way back home.

But sometimes, late at night in her bed, she admitted another truth.

If Cayetano had kissed her like that in a "MIDWEST IS BEST" T-shirt, what would happen when he saw her like this? Dressed like she belonged here? Could it get better than a hurricane?

Yet even as she wondered about kissing him, she couldn't help wondering if, for all his talk about healing the fractures on this island, he wanted to marry her because she looked too much like all the paintings she'd seen reproduced in his books. Of his enemy.

Sometimes the notion made her sad. Other times it made her shiver.

Still other times, she questioned why she was focusing so intently on Cayetano at all when her family tree was just down the side of the mountain…

Each night she would fall asleep resolved, planning to wake up and demand to be taken to Queen Esme. Because she wanted to look in the other woman's face and *not* find herself there.

Yet every morning she woke and made no such demands.

Possibly because, deep down, she was terrified that what she'd see in the Queen's face was the inarguable evidence that they were mother and daughter.

And she already had a mother. Even with Catherine's blessing, it felt like a betrayal.

She spent the bulk of her time with the Signorina. There were usually lunches and teas, during which Delaney learned comportment and manners and customs, and, if it was only the two of them, dissolved into cackles more often than not. When there were others at these meals, Delaney practiced all of the above plus what the Signorina called the *art of conversation*.

"Everybody knows how to talk," Delaney said the first time she brought this up.

"And all they do is talk," the other woman replied. "Talking, talking, talking while the world spirals into wreck and ruin. *Talking* is not an art. It is merely moving your lips so that sounds may escape and collect them into sentences. What you and I are concerned with is conversation, which is not only an art, but a rather underestimated and lost one, in my opinion."

"We're having a conversation right now," Delaney retorted.

The Mediterranean sun streamed down all around them as they sat out in a lush garden, tucked away in one of the private courtyards. Birds sang above them and bees hummed along merrily.

The Signorina set down her teacup and smiled. "And would you categorize the conversation that we're having here as *artful*, dear?"

Delaney was forced to concede the point.

"At the sort of events you will attend in your formal role, one does not talk about oneself," the Signorina told her, holding her teacup aloft.

That was how she liked to refer to Delaney's supposed upcoming wedding. Her *formal role*. And maybe it said something about Delaney that she didn't correct her—but this wasn't the moment to talk about herself, was it?

"It is not the time for personal revelations, confessions, or monologues," the Signorina continued, as if she could read Delaney's mind. "None of that is artful conversation. That is what one saves for one's diary or inflicts upon one's intimates. The point of a good conversation is to engage. The point of the kinds of conversations you may find yourself in, with so many agendas and competing interests, is to entertain without revealing anything you do not wish to reveal. While at the same time trying to make whoever you're speaking to reveal too much. It is very much like a dance."

"I don't dance." Delaney brushed the crumbs of her scone off a dress that probably cost more than her entire previous life. She looked back at her teacher sheepishly. "Maybe that's obvious."

"It is one more thing you and I shall have to remedy," the Signorina said with a laugh. "But first, we will converse, you and I."

And the more they practiced, the more Delaney understood why. It wasn't about the talking. It was a skill, and one she would be expected to use once the world found out who she was. She had no illusions that Cayetano would keep those DNA tests to himself. Whether she married him or not.

She had told Cayetano that she didn't understand the point of pretty rooms filled with all that talking, but now she understood it was in those pretty rooms that a great many decisions were made about what went on outside them. The Signorina was merely teaching her how it was done.

Very much as if she really would be a queen someday.

Her stomach twisted a little more every time she thought such things.

Though she couldn't quite tell if it was panic…or a complicated kind of excitement.

And no matter what it was, it never propelled her into actually *doing* something. She never demanded that she be taken to Cayetano so she could tell him how *she* would like to handle *her* family situation. She never took the opportunity to tell him what he could do with his threats of marriage.

The marriage the Signorina prepared her for every day, as if she wanted to make herself into the warlord's perfect bride.

Sometimes she was tempted to imagine that was what she truly wanted. That she could let herself be swept away by his will alone, and let that be enough, because if she couldn't go back to Kansas and unknow what she'd learned about her parentage…why not be the princess bride of a man who looked at her with burnt gold eyes, dressed her like a queen, and kissed her like a hurricane?

Maybe he was the adventure after all.

One night, two weeks into her time at the castle, Delaney walked to dinner with one of the servants. She knew all their names by now and knew that this one, Ferdinand, was far too overawed by the castle to talk much. She kept catching glimpses of herself in the various mirrors they passed, and it was different, now. *Of course* she had no intention of going through with anything like a wedding, or so she was telling herself tonight, but she no longer saw a stranger in her reflection.

She saw the future Queen all these people were trying—trying *so hard* and she didn't always help, she could admit that—to make her into.

And on nights like this, she thought she could see it, too. She really could almost see it. Because that woman in the mirror looked as alien to a Kansas cornfield as Cayetano had. Delaney thought that really, she looked a bit regal.

She wasn't surprised when Ferdinand led her into a new and different room this particular evening. The Signorina liked to keep things fresh, always moving to a new room, a new group, a new scenario. Training Delaney to stay forever on her toes.

Not that she cared to admit it, but she'd come to like the game.

Delaney was already halfway through the room, the doors closed behind her, when she truly took in the fact that the figure waiting for her tonight was not the diminutive Signorina.

It was Cayetano.

At last.

As if she hadn't learned a thing. As if she

was back in that dusty yard, mystified and too hot, his dark glory almost too hot to bear.

And that suddenly, she was nothing but a farm girl all over again.

CHAPTER EIGHT

CAYETANO COULD SEE the exact moment Delaney registered his presence, because she actually stopped still. Her eyes went wide. It was charming, really. A doe in headlights right here in his private dining room, and his body reacted in what was becoming a predictable way to the little puzzle that was Delaney Clark.

His farm girl who insisted she was no princess when tonight, she looked like a goddess.

That red gown was a wonder, sweeping from one shoulder as if she was competing for a spot in the pantheon. Her black hair was set in a complicated French twist with hints of something sparkly to catch the light.

God, how he wanted her.

That ill-considered kiss had set off a wildfire in him, and even though he'd kept his distance these last two weeks, the sparks remained. One look at her and he could feel them all begin to smolder.

He liked the way she flushed at the sight of him. He liked that he could see exactly how aware she was of him. And he suspected that he was not the only one remembering how that kiss had tasted. And the heat.

That silken, delirious heat that had nearly made him forget himself.

But there was more to concern himself with tonight than the memory of that kiss. For one thing, she no longer in any way resembled that farm girl he'd encountered that day, dirt on her cheeks and all over her clothes.

Her attendants had worked the precise miracle he had entrusted them to perform. There was no hint of overalls and kerchief about her tonight. Her gown skimmed over her figure and made her skin seem to glow. Her hair was not left to the weather and its complex elegance highlighted the fine, inarguably royal features she'd inherited from a long line of Montaignes. That sophisticated nose. Those soaring cheekbones.

He wanted her. This was true. It was always true. He had become uncomfortable with how true it was these last weeks, but tonight it was on another level. She took his breath away.

Because tonight he saw the diamond, not the rough.

And it was a complicated triumph that

pumped through him then. Because Cayetano was attracted to her either way, and the man in him wanted nothing more than to explore her femininity with all the tools at his disposal. His mouth. His hands. His sex.

Until they were both weak with desire.

But the warlord in him, who meant to be King at last, saw his Queen.

And it took more willpower than it should have to stay where he was. To stay put, there at the far end of the room, waiting to see if she would continue to come to him or stay frozen where she was.

Waiting to see what he would do if she stayed put, staring at him as if he was an apparition.

But one that made her cheeks red and her eyes overbright.

He wasn't sure which he would prefer, now that he considered it. Because looking at her was no hardship.

Neither was imagining what he would do with each and every version of her. Farm girl. Vision. Princess. Queen.

And all of them his.

All of them as wild and hot as she'd been in his arms.

It seemed to take her a lifetime or two to straighten her shoulders, then find a practiced sort of smile that he knew came straight from the Signorina. He recognized the particular contours of what the old woman had called her *company smile*.

But he had never wanted to lick a smile like that off anyone's face before.

"This is very disappointing," Delaney said, but she sounded arch and amused, not disappointed. And not really like *Delaney,* either. "The Signorina has been at great pains to tell me that you're an excellent conversationalist. Yet all I get is glowering."

"I'm looking at you, this is true. But I am not glowering."

"Did you know that conversation is an art?" Her smile deepened. "It seems you and I have something in common after all. We are both of us artless."

And that caught him so completely off guard that he laughed.

But, however surprised he might have been at his own laughter, that was nothing next to Delaney's clear astonishment that he was even capable of making such a sound.

She looked...spellbound.

He had not intended to move from where he stood and yet he found himself crossing the room. When he reached her side he took her hand, perhaps because the last time he'd done so, she had looked equally astonished. In the same way she did now, shot through with heat and awareness and the same kind of wonder he could not help but feel when he looked at her.

He led her not to the table that waited for them, but out through the doors to the wide balcony that let in the cool spring night. The stars were already out, thick in the night sky. The valley was inky black below them, the lights in the villages soft, buttery clusters against the dark. The air was not warm, but it was soft as it moved over them.

Usually, Cayetano took this view as seriously as he did everything else. Every point of light he saw before him represented a swathe of people. His people. He had spent years standing here, renewing his commitment to them. Night after night, he had rededicated himself to the cause.

But tonight he let himself marinate in the sweetness of this moment he had often worried would never come. His very own princess in his castle, his wedding in a couple of weeks, his future finally secured.

And through him, his people's destiny forever changed.

Justice was winning. After all these centuries. And it was all because of her.

He had been delighted to find his lost princess, particularly when so many had been certain she didn't—couldn't—exist. He would have brought her here no matter what. But tonight Delaney had transformed herself. She had made herself his dream come true.

Cayetano doubted that had been her goal, or if she'd even had one, but she had done it all the same.

He could not help but take a moment to bask in it. In her.

There were lanterns lit all around, and he liked the way the soft light played over her face.

"What I cannot understand," he said quietly, as if not to disturb the dark, "is how no one in that cornfield of yours recognized the fact that you could not possibly be one of them."

That was as much a statement of fact as some kind of compliment, so he was unprepared when she frowned. "I don't know what you mean."

"Look at you." He was still holding her hand as they stood there against the railing. He indulged himself with his free hand and traced the curve of her cheek. "Your sculpted and aristocratic lines. The House of Montaigne is in your face. It is unmistakable."

"The funny thing about that," she said, in a voice that made it very clear that she did not think anything was particularly funny, "is that what I look like is a Clark. Salt of the earth.

Kansas through and through. The freckles on my nose come from working in the Kansas sun. I have calluses on my hands that are there thanks to Kansas dirt and stubborn Kansas fields. Until you showed up, anyone who'd ever known me would've laughed at the notion that I could ever be anything but a Clark."

Cayetano managed to keep his sigh in check. "I understand this is difficult for you." He did not, in fact, understand. But what could it harm him to say otherwise? He was not precisely lauded for his empathy, but he cast about for some now. "It cannot be easy to be so far from your home, thrust into unfamiliar surroundings, and expected to behave according to others' wishes. I do not envy you."

Her frown eased somewhat. But then it turned speculative. "Is that what it was like for you? When you were sent off to boarding school at a young age?" He must have stared, because she blinked. "The majordomo told me all kinds of history. Some of it was yours."

Cayetano felt himself tense, but tried to dismiss it. "If there were hardships, they pale in comparison to the hardships my people have suffered."

Normally when he said things like that, anyone who heard him started nodding vigorously, because the cause was always paramount—and especially for him. No one actually said *amen,* but it was implied.

Delaney did neither. If anything, she looked quizzical. "It's not like suffering is a pie and if one person gets a piece no one else can have some. Tragically, there's always enough to go around."

Cayetano felt something inside him...tilt and go precarious, suddenly. He didn't understand what it was. "I don't believe I attempted to quantify suffering."

"It's what you do, though, isn't it?" She phrased that as a question, yet did not appear to actually be asking. "You never actually talk about your feelings. You talk about your country."

"My country matters," Cayetano retorted. His fingers tightened, ever so slightly, on hers. "My feelings do not."

She looked down at their joined hands as if there was some significance there that he had missed. He found himself looking, too, and was furious with himself.

"Is it that your feelings don't matter or that you don't know how to identify them?"

"What is the Signorina teaching you?" And he recognized the new sensation rising inside him. It was as if he was preparing for battle. He felt the way he sometimes did, honed and

ready, as if at any moment he would be required
to fight to the death.

Not the physical battles of his ancestors,
swords and blood. His battles had mostly been
in the press. But the preparation within him
was the same. And he always landed his blows.

And there was a very specific battle he
wished to undertake with this woman—but it
was not this one. And it was not about blows,
but passion.

"You look angry," Delaney observed with
maddening calm.

"I doubt that very much," he managed to
reply, with a reasonable facsimile of calm.
Through his teeth. "I cannot get angry. As
policy."

"Says the man who identifies himself as a
warlord, angrily."

"Warlord is a title." Cayetano made himself
smile. Or curve his lips, anyway. "A title I take
seriously. A warlord cannot afford anger. Not
in these uncertain times."

She tilted her head to one side, her blue eyes
seeing far too much. "Do you actually know
when you're angry?"

And it was suddenly as if everything inside
of him was jumbled all around and out of place.
He felt out of control again, and he wasn't even

touching her the way he wanted to do. He could not abide the *mess* of it.

Or the fact that it was more than that madness that had overtaken him when he'd kissed her before. It was as if she'd reached inside him and threw everything out of place, and he couldn't understand how that could be. He was a fortress. And while this was an odd conversation, it was innocuous. Surely it was no more than idle talk.

Yet inside him, the call to battle kept sounding.

Cayetano attempted to settle himself down in the usual way, by thinking about their upcoming wedding. Because nothing mattered but that. All roads led to that ceremony.

"Plans for our wedding are well underway," he told her. Gruffly.

And only when she drew her hand from his, then crossed her arms, did he understand that he had deliberately changed the subject so that she could be the one on the defensive here.

He couldn't say he liked what that said about him.

"The wedding of the warlord would normally be an international affair," he said, pushing forward despite the way she was regarding him. "We have many allies in different countries and we usually like them to take part in our rituals.

It legitimizes them. Not that we require legitimacy, but it does make claims to the contrary from the palace below more difficult."

He trusted that the majordomo had done his job and Delaney knew that *the palace below* was how his people had referred to the seat of the Montaigne family's power, sitting pretty in its own rocky cove on the island's prettiest beach.

Because of course it did.

"No one's consulted me about any wedding plans." And while her tone was still calm, Cayetano could easily read the temper in her gaze.

"Why would they?" he asked, finding it far easier to make himself appear at ease now that it was her temper on the rise. "You have far too much on your plate as it is. Learning to accept your new role. Exploring your new home."

Becoming his Queen.

She glared at him. "I think that if there are wedding plans, they should include the bride. That seems reasonable, doesn't it? Otherwise it starts to look a lot like you're hiding something. Or plotting something."

"Anyone can be a bride, Delaney." He was enjoying himself now, even if, somewhere deep inside, where everything seemed to have found its place again, he questioned himself and his motives. And deeper still, he wondered why it was that only she managed to penetrate all the shields he'd spent his whole life nailing into place. "All a bride need do is appear at the wedding. But not everyone can train to become the next Queen of Ile d'Montagne."

Then he watched as she clearly wrestled with her reaction to the idea of becoming Queen. Very clearly. Very obviously.

He found it more intriguing than he should have.

"One thing at a time," she said after a moment, though her eyes darkened. "First I need to become a bride. I should focus on that. Something that would be easier to do if I was actually included in my own wedding plans."

"And by *focus on that* do you mean you wish to actually plan our wedding?" He wanted to touch her again, so he did, reaching over to run his hand down the length of one bare arm, delighting in the way she shivered at the contact. And the goose bumps that marked the path he'd taken. "Or do you mean you would like to obstruct any wedding plans so that they never come to pass?"

He hadn't intended to accuse her, or not so directly. It had been more of an idle question, really, because he knew what she did not—that nothing would stop their wedding. This was Ile d'Montagne and he was the warlord. It was his vow that made them one, not her compliance.

But he opted not to share that nugget of ancient law with her. Because it made sense to wait, to create a scene that could be extensively photographed and beamed around the world. To make sure valley artisans made a dress that was worthy of a queen.

To make sure that she was already considered a queen before he made it clear to everyone that she would be the next one here.

Yet her response showed him that the question was not idle at all. Her cheeks bloomed a new red. And she looked as guilty as if he'd caught her in the middle of a desperate act.

"I'm shocked," he drawled. When, in truth, he was charmed. Captivated. It should have worried him more than it did. "Do you truly imagine you can scheme against me?"

"You said I had a month. It's been two weeks. Barely."

"I said the wedding would be in a month and so it shall be." She made as if to argue and he shrugged. "You knew the choices before you, Delaney. Perhaps I should remind you that at any time I can make my claim upon you. We do not need to plan a wedding at all."

"No," she said hurriedly, and maybe there was something wrong with him that he took such pleasure in the panic in her gaze. "I want to plan it. That's all I meant."

"You're a liar, little one."

But he couldn't muster up the sense of outrage that should have accompanied a statement like that. He, who prized honesty so dearly. There was something about the genuine distress in her blue eyes that made it impossible.

"Cayetano," she said, sounding as if she was working very hard to consider each word carefully. Or maybe she wanted to taste his name as much as he liked to taste hers. "I don't want you to get the wrong idea. I'm not lying. Or I don't mean to lie. But you want me to accept two overwhelming things, and you want that acceptance immediately."

She paused, as if waiting for him to argue, but all he did was incline his head.

Delaney let out a shaky breath, then continued. "One overwhelming thing is that I'm not the person I thought I was my entire life. That instead, I'm this completely *other* person, who is meant to live in places like this and has to worry about *artful conversation* as a potential weapon of diplomacy when what I know is corn. And the other is your apparent belief that it's perfectly reasonable to marry a total stranger. It's only been fourteen days, Cayetano. That's not enough time. For acceptance. For anything."

He settled in against the railing, studying her lovely face. She didn't need the cosmetics she wore, but he liked the way they enhanced her natural beauty. The truth was, he liked every version of her that he'd encountered so far. Including this one tonight.

The one who spoke of needing more time when the Signorina reported that she came to her daily lessons eagerly. And enjoyed herself, by all accounts. Almost as if she'd already accepted more than she wanted to admit.

To herself.

"And what amount of time do you imagine it would require for you to make yourself easy about both of these things?" he asked her.

She dropped her arms and opened her palms to the sky. "A year? Five years? A lifetime?"

"I sympathize." And the strange thing was that he did. But it would not save her. "And yet you must know that these things cannot wait."

"Maybe not forever." Her voice was a whisper. Her eyes had gone big in the lantern light as she pled her case. "But surely they can wait a little while."

The strangest sensation washed over him then, more shocking to him than if he'd suddenly lost his footing and plummeted over the steep side of the castle walls. It was something about how plaintive her voice was. Or how wide her eyes were. Maybe it was her voice. All of it. None of it. How could he tell?

Maybe it was the simple fact of her, so unlike any other woman he'd ever known, with her talk of dirt and calluses on the one hand and her interest in his bloody feelings on the other. When what he was used to was simpering and flattery and attempts to spend more time in his bed than he wished. From women who apparently failed to comprehend that he was actually a man, flesh and blood and possessed of a few stray thoughts that did not involve the cause.

His own people had never seen into him like this woman did.

No one ever had.

It should have been dizzying. Perhaps it was. Perhaps that was this new sensation inside— a kind of mad intoxication that would lead to peril, whether he toppled over the walls or lost himself the way his parents had.

But he rather thought instead it was something far more curious.

There was a part of him that wanted to give her time. That wanted her to find her way into this. To meet him here.

Yes, they were strangers. Yes, this was swift, and there were a thousand reasons not to marry in haste and only one reason to go ahead—a reason that had nothing to do with her, save a trick of DNA and a careless hospital.

Yet the part of him that wanted to give her time was the part that didn't care about any of that. It cared that at the root of it all, he wanted her.

He had set eyes on her in that yard, before he'd even exited his car, and he'd wanted her.

The way normal men must want, he'd thought at the time. With so much desperation and uncertainty when he should have been filled instead with purpose. Because she was the answer to generations of prayers.

She was his endgame.

And still he wanted to wait. Not so he could stage a wedding that would captivate the imaginations of the world as he was doing now. What he was doing now made sense. This urge in him to let her find her way to him was a traitor.

Because you want her to want you, came a voice within. *Not the warlord of this valley, the true King of this island. But you. Cayetano. The man.*

But that was a treachery he did not intend to allow this night. It was far too seismic to take on.

"I'm sympathetic to the whiplash you must feel, given your change in circumstances," he told her, hoping he gave no hint of his inner turmoil. Or how desperately he wanted her in all the ways he shouldn't. "It cannot be easy to have the world you know swept from beneath you so swiftly. I cannot apologize for it, but I do understand it can't be easy."

She looked at him for a long while, there in the darkness with only the lantern light between them. It made everything seem closer. Warmer.

It made him wonder if *feeling* was not so terrible after all.

"I suppose I am trying to think of it all as a gift," she said, as if she was confessing. As if it was not easy to get out the words. "It's not a gift I would have chosen. But it's better to know the truth than live a lie, right?" She let out a laugh, though it was rueful. "That's what my grandmother always said."

"She sounds a wise woman," Cayetano said.

He chose not to point out that her actual grandmother had been the icy Queen Carlota, notable for both her cruelty and her voracious appetites. Not a font of wisdom, the little-mourned Carlota.

But he kept that to himself.

And felt virtuous in his restraint.

"I can't say that I'm coming to terms with it, exactly," Delaney told him in the same confessional tone. "It helps that every time I try to call my mother, she's too busy setting up her new life to talk to me for more than five minutes. And she sounds happy. Two weeks ago she barely had a life. For that alone, I guess I'm grateful."

"Then perhaps, little one, you do not need so many years after all."

"Accepting that it's true isn't the same thing as accepting it's who I am." Delaney pulled in a breath and straightened her shoulders, and the way she looked at him changed. Intensified, maybe. "But it's the other part that I'm more worried about. Because what I accept or don't accept doesn't have a time limit, does it? But this wedding of yours does."

"You said that your primary objection is marrying a stranger," Cayetano reminded her. "But I'm not so strange, am I?"

That fine line between her brows made an appearance. "I don't know you at all."

"You know the most important things." He inclined his head. "You know that I need you, which gives you power."

If he'd expected that to make her easy, he was disappointed. She scowled at him.

"When my grandmother used to talk about falling in love with my grandfather, she talked about a lot of things. How quiet he was with everyone except her. How he looked at her as if she was prettier every day. The nicknames that were only theirs. She never once mentioned *power* unless it was a story about waiting out a tornado." Delaney shook her head. At him. "Weirdly, she was much more focused on love."

Once again, he was struck by how much he liked the sheen of temper in her gaze. He wanted to taste her fire. He wanted a woman who could handle his own. He could not help but think this all boded well.

Despite this talk of feelings.

"Love is a wondrous thing, or so I'm told," he said dismissively. "But it is not all things. Love is blind, but with the power you already possess, you also know certain truths. I cannot harm you, for how would that look? The eyes of the world will be upon us the moment your true status is known. That makes you safe. I assume it is why you came with me so easily."

She did not nod along enthusiastically to that. On the contrary, her eyes narrowed, and she looked at him as if he didn't make sense. "It hadn't actually occurred to me to be worried about my safety. Until now."

"Then you are even more sheltered than I imagined." He could hear that his voice had gone rough. "What could possibly be more important than your safety?"

Delaney laughed a little, and looked something like dazed. "When you put it that way, it does seem silly. But I've always felt safe." She shook her head slightly. "Even though it's very clear to me that you are by far the most dangerous man I've ever met."

There was something so innocent in the way she said that. It nearly unmanned him. Because she did not seem to understand the great compliment she was giving him.

And he could not bear to tell her.

Though turned out, he could not bear to let it slide by unremarked, either. "I will never hurt you, Delaney," he managed to grit out. "Know this, if nothing else."

She nodded, slowly, as if she was busy considering him. "Cayetano. Why would you think that my expectation is that you would hurt me?"

Once again, this all seemed to be inching a little too close to topics he did not discuss. Ever. "I only wish to make you feel easy about the choice before you."

"Is that it?" That blue gaze seemed to see straight through him, again. When he had always considered himself opaque. He had reveled in it, in fact. "Because this is starting to seem as if it's a great deal more personal."

But Cayetano thought only of the history of his people. Not his history. Not his family.

Not the choices that had been made when he was too young to have a voice.

Not the things that had happened that he'd been unable to prevent. The wild, raging displays that were his legacy—the legacy he had decidedly turned his back on.

All in the name of one love or another, so that the word itself was suspect.

He spoke of none of this.

And still his heart hammered against his ribs, as if he was that young boy once again. Trapped in the decisions of others so far away from home.

"I'm glad you've given no thought to your safety," he told her silkily. "That either makes you very foolish or me very trustworthy. I choose to believe it is both."

"Wait—" she began.

"The fact of the matter is this," he said, cutting her off, no longer worried that he might sound too forbidding. Too ruthless. He was both. "It is not that I dislike the modern take on marriage. I am modern myself in many ways. But falling in love, getting to know another, and wasting so much time… These might seem like virtues, perhaps, on a farm. In this Kansas of yours. But here we speak not of cornfields, but kingdoms. And you already know all you need to know. I am not brutal. I have vowed not to harm you and I have not. In cases like ours, this should be enough."

"Maybe that's enough for you. It's not enough for me."

And she lifted her chin while she said that, clearly not recognizing that doing that only made her more beautiful to him. Because he was not brutal, that was true. But he was still a warlord. He liked the battle. It was only that the battleground had changed in this modern era. He did not intend to fight Queen Esme on horseback, surrounded by warriors. He did not intend to use his hands. But his future wife?

Well. He would use the weapons he had.

"Do you want romance?" he asked her. "Love?"

He had been taking care not to sound mocking, but she still jerked her head away as if he'd slapped at her. "And if I say yes?" Her eyes flashed. "What then? Will you start spouting poetry?"

"I have already given you a sample of the only poetry I know," Cayetano told her, dark and low. "And if memory serves, my little farm girl, you loved it."

"You have never given me a poem." She glared in that way that sent a bolt of pure desire straight to his sex. "I think I would remember."

"Memories are so fickle," he murmured.

Cayetano reached over and hooked his hand around her neck. He pulled her close, taking a deep pleasure in the way her lips parted immediately. The way heat and awareness bloomed in her gaze. And the way she melted into him as if this edgy, encompassing wanting was in her, too. As if it had claimed them both.

"Pay attention, Delaney," he told her. "This is a sonnet."

And then he fit his mouth to hers once more.

CHAPTER NINE

DELANEY HAD STUDIED poetry in high school like everybody else. She wasn't any kind of expert on the subject. But one thing she did know was that no poem she'd ever read for English class had exploded inside her like this.

It was different from that kiss her first afternoon here.

Better. Wilder.

He kissed her and he kissed her, his hard mouth making her feel fluttery, everywhere. Parts of her that shouldn't have fluttered at all couldn't seem to stop. Maybe she was the flutter. And maybe she didn't care. She felt reckless and sure as his hard mouth claimed hers again and again.

She meant to push him away, because surely she should *want* to push him away, but instead her hands got tangled on him. Lost somewhere in the sweep of his wide, hard chest. Her fingers curled around the lapels of the suit he wore, and she relished the fact that she could cling to something. Anything.

Because everything else was a storm of sensation. It pounded through her. It stole her away and redeemed her anew as his tongue stroked hers. It was all pulse and heartbeat, sensation and need.

She hadn't known that a person could ache like this, filled with an almost pain for something she couldn't even name. It felt like a prayer.

Delaney kept thinking, when she could think at all, that she hadn't known what she was missing.

On and on he kissed her with what she could tell, even half out of her mind, was both consummate skill and an edgy sort of passion. Something in her recognized it. Thrilled to it.

Wanted it—and him—all the more.

Something in her cracked open, wider and wider with every touch of his tongue to hers.

As if this was her true homecoming. His hands on her neck. His mouth on hers. And the storm that she thought she'd be perfectly happy to see rage on forever as long as he kept kissing her like this.

Like he might die if he stopped.

His scent was all around her now. It was indefinably male and entirely him. She wondered if later, if she survived this, she would be unable to breathe without the scent careening through her.

And even imagining that made it better. The intensity seemed brighter.

She shuddered, low and long.

And for some reason, that made him laugh in much the same way.

For a moment, she remembered herself. Her goals—or the fact that she ought to have had goals these last two weeks. She should have demanded to be taken to meet her biological relative at the very least. But she hadn't. Every day she'd meant to make that stand, but she hadn't.

Maybe this was why. She could see only Cayetano, and beyond him, the stars.

She could only see him and ever since she'd laid eyes on him at the farm, he was all she wanted to see. Here, now, she could finally admit that.

This was what she wanted. Or no matter what Catherine had said to her about *adventure,* she would never have gotten in that car.

There were more complicated reasons she hadn't forced the issue of meeting the Queen. That hadn't changed.

But there was also this.

There was Cayetano.

And this magical, marvelous fire between them that burned hotter by the moment.

When he pulled her close again, then hauled her up even further so he could hold her in his arms, all she could do was melt.

This time, he kissed her with all the wondrous desperation from before. She met him with the same yearning, the same fire.

But this time, as their lips tangled, the hand that wasn't gripping her and holding her to him...traveled.

Down her bared shoulder, then to the bodice of her dress, unerringly finding her breast and lifting it out. He broke off from the kiss again, but before she could think to protest the loss, he bent his head. Shifting her as he held her there—outside, where presumably anyone could see them if they had a view of his balcony, and why didn't she care?—he bent his mouth to her breast instead.

And when his lips closed on her nipple, proud and taut, it was as if all the stars in the sky above her crashed into her.

She let her head fall back. Her hands were fists on his shoulders.

But Cayetano...slowed down.

He slowed down, and then, if she wasn't mistaken and it was her own pounding heart, he growled.

Then he did it again, and there was no confusing it. It was a profoundly male sound. It seemed to crash through her like so many stars, but they all landed deeper. Lower.

And one by one, began to burn there, low in her belly.

She had the notion, intense and beautiful, that he was devouring her. Eating her alive where they stood.

His mouth kept working at her breasts, and she arched her back so she could better offer herself to him. So she could be certain that he didn't miss a single part of her.

Because she would have sworn in this moment that she had been born for this.

For him.

She was so consumed with what he was doing that she almost missed the way his hand tracked lower, finding her hip and the outside of her thigh where the fabric of the dress parted. His mouth moved against her nipples, one and then the other, but his hand found the roundness of her bottom and squeezed tight.

That, too, was a storm.

Too many storms to name.

And then everything felt tinged with red, hectic and stunning at once, as that same hand reversed track, but this time beneath the skirt of her dress.

It seemed as if she couldn't quite take in the sensation that moved through her. She couldn't catalog it. She could only ride it out. His wonderful, devilish mouth. The arm that held her up and the hand that gripped her side. And below, his marvelously strong fingers as they traced a path—slowly, agonizingly, beautifully—up along the inside of her thigh.

She thought she might die when he finally reached the soft heat between her thighs.

But she didn't. Delaney had never felt so alive.

Bristling with need, beautiful and impossibly lush—

Cayetano continued into her wet heat, circling the center of her need until she found herself making the strangest keening noises. Then, with a twist of his wrist, he plunged deep within.

His thumb found her outside while his finger stroked deep within. His mouth stayed busy at her breast. Everything was fire and a tugging wet heat, and then she had absolutely no choice.

No choice and no fight in her.

Delaney didn't so much fall apart as fly.

She became stars, all of them at once, and it was hot and, oh, so bright.

It was him, Cayetano, in all his dark glory.

And she was certain of only one thing as

she burst bright and then became so many torn apart pieces that she felt she was made of stars herself.

She would never be the same again.

But he gave her no time to contemplate what that might mean. She was dimly aware that he set her back on her feet. Even tucked her breasts back into place with a surprising gentleness, and then, without a single word from her—because she could hardly speak and wouldn't know what to say—he ushered her back into his dining room. And seated her. So that they shared the corner of the table.

And by the time she blinked herself fully awake and aware again, the food was served.

Delaney hardly knew what to do with herself. She hadn't noticed the servants' arrival and was only dimly aware when they withdrew. And Cayetano seemed not to notice that she merely sat there, undone. Completely and totally undone. Or maybe he did notice, she amended a moment later, because he served her as well as him.

And everything on her plate made her mouth water, but how to concentrate on food? That wasn't what she was hungry for.

She still felt as if everything in her was simmering along, coming closer and closer to a boil. Her body felt like it no longer belonged to her. As if the way he had touched her, so masterful, so certain, had altered her. Inside and out.

Her thoughts spooled out in her head like songs. Like a melody she couldn't quite catch. The burnt gold of his eyes. What he'd said about her safety when she worried about his. That impossible storm he brewed in her, and how eagerly she'd leaped over an edge she had never known was there.

There had been no edges in Kansas. No cliffs.

She watched him eat in silence, the heat in her rising and rising, cresting toward that boil as her own body seemed to work against her—or maybe with her—

But when he looked over at her, his gaze was darker. Knowing. And that mouth of his that she'd now tasted and learned and craved… curved.

She felt as struck as if he'd hit her. She wanted to jump to her feet and announce what was so obvious to her. That she wasn't the same woman who'd walked into this room feeling like a queen. That her entire *being* was different. That she had changed, profoundly, and how could he *eat dinner*?

This was yet another edge and she'd already

gone hurtling off the side. He should have seen her, catapulting out into space.

Delaney thought she might explode. Or maybe she already had. Maybe that was the trouble. Maybe that was where all the commotion inside her came from.

Her problem was, she had no idea where it was going to go.

"I've never actually had sex," she announced.

Which summed up everything and nothing. It was just awkward and embarrassing. When inside her, what she'd wanted to say was all elegance and lyricism.

She instantly wanted to snatch those words back, particularly when they seemed to land with such a loud *thunk* in the middle of the brightly tiled mosaic table.

But then again, perhaps not, because the heat in Cayetano's mythic gaze...shifted.

And Delaney felt a different sort of warmth move through her, almost as if this bizarre night had turned...affectionate.

Don't kid yourself, she lectured herself sternly. *You know exactly what this man's interest is in you.*

"You have my condolences," Cayetano said after a long moment that felt breathless to her. "That seems an unfortunate oversight."

"If I had a boyfriend at all, it was the farm,"

Delaney told him, still trying to find her feet beneath her. She was glad she was sitting down. "And besides, I never understood how my friends from high school were suddenly able to overlook the fact that the boys in our class when we were seventeen were the same boys in our class from when we were six. With much the same issues in the way of personal hygiene and questionable behavior." She wrinkled up her nose. "It seemed like everyone had amnesia, but I didn't."

Cayetano did not comment on the dearth of acceptable suitors back home. Instead, he filled her wineglass with something rich and red, that smelled to her of currants and honey. The one other time she'd tried wine it had been from an illicit box at a high school friend's bachelorette party, and it had been notable for its grittiness and sour taste. But when she pressed this glass to her lips, the kiss of his wine warmed her almost the way he did, leaving a kind of yearning on her tongue.

"I don't drink much, either," she said very solemnly over the rim of her glass. "So if this is an attempt to loosen me up, well… It's going to work."

"Excellent."

His intense eyes crinkled in the corners and that made her feel as if she was turning cartwheels when she knew she was sitting still. He reached across the corner of the table that separated them and pulled on one of the tendrils that had fallen free from the rest of her hair, tied back in such a complicated arrangement it had taken all of her servants to make it work.

And she probably shouldn't have allowed him to toy with her hair. Or with her. But she was still hot and molten between her legs. There were still all those sensations charging around inside of her. Her breasts were so oversensitized that she felt shooting streaks of electricity every time she breathed. So all she did was cup her wineglass between her hands, take another, deeper sip, and carry on talking.

"I expected to get married someday," she told him. He was curling that strand of hair around and around his finger, tugging it slightly, and somehow that made everything between them just that little bit dizzy. "But all I cared about was the farm, you see. So it couldn't be just anyone. It had to be another farmer, and how do you find a farmer who's willing to farm your land, not his?"

Again, that lift at the corners of his eyes. As good as a belly laugh from another man. "I am afraid, little one, that I am not conversant on the intricacies of farmland dating in the American heartland."

She registered his dry tone, and for some reason that made her laugh. "But don't you see? I grant you, the scope is different. But at the end of the day, both you and I want to marry for land. You just think yours matters more."

Cayetano stilled. This close, she could see an arrested sort of light dawn in his eyes. And it was so strange how actually reading him made all these various sensations inside her seem to pull tighter and tighter.

As if this was what she'd wanted from the start.

To know the impossibly beautiful man, sculpted to perfection, who never should have set foot on the farm. To *know* him in every way a person could know another.

He stared back at her for a long while. Then his gaze shuttered, and he shifted to pull one of her hands into his. It felt new and almost sacred to sit there, hushed like this. Hot. To watch as he bent his head, his gaze on their linked hands while his thumb made slow, sweet sweeps against her skin.

"You're quite right," he said, and when she felt a jolt deep inside her she realized that this was a surprise, too. That she'd expected him to argue. To rant and rave about history and Montaignes and false queens.

"I beg your pardon?"

He looked up then, his expression rueful. "I said you were right. You are. It is not for me to decide the importance of the things that matter to you. My understanding is that this farm of yours is being sold."

Her throat was much too dry, suddenly. "It seems my mother found it a burden."

"And you did not?"

Delaney sighed. She hadn't been gone from Kansas long, she knew that. And yet still, the fact that she was gone at all made everything different. That was the thing about perspective, she supposed. You only recognized how little you'd had when you happened upon some.

"I would never have called it a burden," she told him, and she was aware that she had never been this honest before. Not with anyone. Not even with herself, because it would have felt like a betrayal. "It's just… That's what love is, isn't it? You put in the work because it's worth it, because you love it. Not because it will ever love you back. You work the land because that's what you do. Because you're a farmer who lives on a farm. And nothing could ever change that, or so I thought, so it never occurred to me to think in terms of whether or not it made me happy. How can you know that you're carrying a burden until you put it down and see how much it's weighed all this time?"

Again, that arrested look. And she could see something, there on his face of stone, but it was gone in the next instant.

But she knew what she'd seen. For a moment he'd almost looked…raw.

"There's absolutely no reason that you can't hold on to that land if you wish it," he said, roughly. His attention was on her linked hands again. "I will instruct my people to buy it tomorrow. It is easy enough to hire someone to tend to it."

"But it's not mine," she said quietly. And then, though it hurt, "it was never mine. If my mother doesn't want it, then it must belong instead to Princess Amalia."

Cayetano let out a derisive sound. "There is no possibility on this earth that a spoiled princess like Amalia will ever wish to dirty her hands. And certainly not somewhere so far away from the beaches of Positano or St. Tropez."

"Perhaps a princess would not." Delaney kept her gaze trained on him. "But she's not a princess, is she?"

And something seemed to swell between them. It wasn't as simple as heat. She almost wanted to call it something else, something more like *vulnerable*—

But Cayetano made another noise, this one a

deep rumble of need that seemed to lodge itself deep inside her. And then he was moving from his chair, sweeping her up from her seat and into his arms, pausing only to fuse his mouth to hers once more.

There was a part of her that wanted to protest, because she was sure that something momentous had happened here. And that if they only stayed *right here*, in this odd little moment where she was sure she could see parts of him he normally hid, they could make something kindle to life—

But his kiss was hard and hot, demanding her focus. Commanding her full attention.

She hardly knew what was happening when he began to move, carrying her out onto the balcony again. But he didn't stop there. He continued walking, still holding her aloft, before shouldering his way in through a different set of doors.

His bedroom, she understood in a haze as he laid her down on the high, imposing bed, and settled himself half beside her and half on top of her.

And then he kissed her more. Deeper. Harder. In a way that made it clear that he'd been holding himself back before.

This was different. This was raw, unchained. *Beautiful,* something in her whispered.

And he built the same storm, leading her even more quickly this time toward the same edge.

Delaney had some faint presence of mind as he helped her out of her dress, growling in deep male appreciation as he found her breasts, then slipped her panties from her hips. She was aware of every moment, of every part of her that he bared with his hands, then gazed at with such delicious possessiveness. He lavished her with heat and need, stirring her to a fever pitch. Then he tossed her over the side again, this time not waiting for her to shudder back to earth.

Instead he moved further south to settle himself between her legs.

That time she screamed when she flew apart, as the warlord ate her alive.

He rolled away from her then to strip out of his own clothes, and she felt almost uncomfortably torn. There was the spectacle of his beautiful male body, somehow even more glorious out of his clothes than in them. But at the same time, she couldn't help thinking how mad this was. How unlike her.

Was she really about to do this thing that for twenty-four years had never been so much as the faintest blip on her radar?

Yes, he was beautiful. Yes, he seemed like

more of a man to her than every other man she'd ever met, put together.

But this was so out of character.

He stood over her, there by the side of the bed, his eyes blazing and every line and muscle of his body held taut.

"You are already mine," he told her, his voice low and dark, like a stirring deep inside her own soul. "You are the answer to prayer. The hope of a people. This is already so, little one. But tonight, you understand, the gift of your innocence and the fact you give it to me changes everything."

"You're too late," she whispered, and it was odd that she had no sense of shame. No urge to cover herself when she had always been so modest. On the contrary, she felt wild with her own power and sat up, offering herself to him even more fully. "Everything is already changed. What's one more thing?"

And finally, Cayetano laughed. He laughed and laughed, and she understood with a deep kind of shock, a wild sort of thrill, that she had known this man so short a time. Almost no time at all, and yet would do anything for that laughter.

Anything for him, something in her whispered.

But maybe she already knew that.

Or she never would have come here.

And she certainly never would have found herself naked with this man.

She felt as unsteady as she had on the plane, but this time, he was with her. This time, she could reach and touch him, and that made all the difference. She didn't need ground beneath her feet, not when the burnt gold of his gaze seemed to cover her in all that molten heat.

As if she was made of the same stuff.

"I have already claimed you for my country, Delaney," he growled at her. He moved over her then, climbing onto the bed and lowering himself so that he pressed her down, his flesh against hers, and it was extraordinary. He braced his hands on either side of her head, holding her face where he wanted it. "But tonight, little one, I also claim you for me."

She felt him between her legs, huge and hard, and she caught her breath—whether to cheer or sob or laugh wildly herself, she would never know.

It was all molten and gold straight through.

Because with a twist of his hips he thrust himself deep. And she was soft and needy still, but yet she felt that sharp tug—

She gasped, but it was gone in an instant.

And his mouth was at her neck while he began to move, inexorable, inescapable, and so shockingly beautiful that she didn't understand how anything could possibly feel this excruciatingly perfect—

But with every thrust of the hardest part of him deep into the heart of her heat, it got better.

When that should have been impossible.

She felt raw, exposed. And at the same time, closer to this man than she had ever been to another in her life.

He was inside her. But she felt as if she was inside him, too.

Cayetano held her against him, and she arched up so she could press herself against the wall of his chest. So she could take him deeper and deeper still. And the color of his eyes was as molten she felt—

And then everything was bright and too hot and shattering.

It went on forever.

But this time they broke apart together.

And it was a long while later when she found her way back to herself again, drowsy and inordinately pleased to find herself tucked up against his side. She could hear his breathing. His scent was all around her. She was delightfully warm though there were no covers over her.

It was only when she thought about looking for one that she realized he had never turned on a light when they'd come inside. That meant that she could lie there, his heavy arm around her and her head on his magnificent chest, and look out and see nothing but stars. Brilliant, beautiful.

As mysterious and unknowable as he was.

But even as she thought that a different sort of melody wound its way through her. Because everything was changed again. He was right about that. What had happened tonight had made too many things abundantly clear to her. But maybe because of that, something had occurred to her.

Because it was true, everything that had happened since he'd pulled up in the yard was out of character for Delaney Clark, farm girl from Kansas, who never had seen beyond the cornfields.

But that wasn't who she was. Like it or not, she was a princess. One day she would be Queen.

His Queen.

When he shifted beside her, she turned to find that he was wide-awake, the burnt gold of his eyes simmering.

And before he could speak she reached over and traced a finger over that hard, starkly sensual mouth.

She couldn't say what she wanted to say.

What it hurt her not to say, with all her heart. It was too soon. Too new.

I love you, she wanted to shout. To cry. To sing.

But she couldn't say it out loud. Not yet.

So she said the next best thing instead.

"I will marry you," Delaney whispered. Not that he had been in any doubt, she knew that. But it was different for her to say it. And she could see the way it lit him up. She could feel the heavy male part of him stir against her. So she held his gaze, even as she reached her hand down to curl her fingers around that silken steel. She shuddered in anticipation, but held his gaze so there could be no mistake. "Cayetano, I will be your Queen."

CHAPTER TEN

THE DAY OF the wedding dawned blue and bright at last. Cayetano had barely slept.

And not for the usual reasons these days.

He allowed himself a smile where he stood, aware that such things as smiles came easier these days. He had dispensed with Delaney's guest quarters and had her moved into his the morning after the night she'd given herself to him, because he hadn't wanted to waste a single moment more. It wasn't just her body, that lush wonder, that called to him, though it did. It was her.

Cayetano hungered for the stories she told him, at first haltingly and then, when he asked for more tales of the alien place she'd come from, with a little theater. He longed for the wisdom wrapped up in the tart sayings she ascribed to her grandmother, so different from his own experience with family. And more and more he found he craved the steady way she listened and the calm way she talked, proving to him with every passing day that no one could possibly be more perfect for what lay ahead.

The future might be rocky as they claimed their rightful place. He knew that. But these last two weeks had been a revelation.

He might even call them a joy, had anyone dared to ask.

He would have married her and made her his Queen no matter what, but it pleased him that the Signorina reported nothing but stellar progress. And more, actually liked the woman she called their perfectly imperfect Queen. All the palace personnel adored her. Delaney had applied herself to her new role with all the determination she must have brought to bear back home, season after thankless season in those fields of hers.

And what time she did not spend preparing herself for what was to come when her identity was released to the world, or telling him her homespun stories because she delighted in making him laugh, she spent in his bed.

It had been only two short weeks and yet Cayetano found he could no longer recall another woman's face. Delaney's taste haunted him. He even found himself drawing the kinds of boundaries he never had before with his men, because he needed to make sure he got back to her as soon as he could. As often as he could.

Soon enough there would be nothing but the cause again, as there had always been, all his life.

And every time he tripped over his own alarms, his own red flags, he reminded himself that he was not his mother. His aim was to fulfill the centuries-long dream of his people, not pervert it to his own ends. And today, as he waited for his bride at last in the grand courtyard of Arcieri Castle, he admitted to himself that it was true. He had lost his head a little these last weeks.

Some part of him was already grieving that these heady, magical days needed to end, but they did.

You could only give yourself so fully because it was temporary, a voice in him said. He wanted to believe it. He really did.

But it didn't matter what he believed. Today was the day that everything changed.

He heard a cheer go up and he took in the sight of so many of his people packed onto all the galleries and balconies, even peering out the windows, all of them there to catch a glimpse of this moment.

This moment that was theirs. It belonged to them, after all this time. There was no foreign press, no dignitaries. There was only Cayetano, warlord only a little while longer, and the lost Montaigne Princess—who appeared in the grand entryway dressed in a snowy white that made the black of her hair and the blue of her eyes seem enchanted.

Or maybe her smile did that.

Still, there was only Delaney, who had insisted that she hold wildflowers picked from the valley floor today, endearing herself to his people forever.

Delaney, who'd given herself to him so fully, and with such innocent delight, that even thinking of her beneath him made something deep within him shudder.

But that, too, was about to change.

He had told himself repeatedly over these last two weeks that this was merely a little breath, that was all. He'd spent his whole life fighting and the better part of these last years searching for her. Today he would marry her. No one could fault him for these too-short weeks of enjoying her before the world found out about her.

But now the day had come. Now, at long last, the throne of Ile d'Montagne was within the grasp of an Arcieri.

Cayetano told himself that he was impatient with this ceremony only because it was the final necessary step before he launched himself straight on into his destiny.

But as his beautiful bride held his hands there at the altar they'd made, and repeated her vows in that lovely voice of hers—gone husky with emotion just as her eyes filled with tears—he accepted another truth, too.

He wanted the coming space between them. Because he was terribly afraid that Delaney wasn't the only one surrendering herself here.

And that was unacceptable. He could not allow himself to falter. He knew what might well become of him if he did.

As the priest intoned the words of the ancient rite, Cayetano found himself searching the windows on the highest level of the castle, looking for the blazing set of eyes he knew all too well.

His mother, trotted out today as an emblem of his enduring mercy. Allowed to attend her son's wedding, but only from afar, lest she take it upon herself to try take her son's place.

Again.

But no matter how many times Cayetano told himself that he was done with his mother and satisfied with where they had ended up, when he saw her again it was as if he'd started from scratch.

It couldn't have been more different from what he shared with Delaney, but something about his mother wedged its way beneath his armor, too.

He jerked his eyes away from hers, focused once more on his bride, and somehow controlled the pulse of impatience inside him. For he had come too far to fall now.

When it was time, Cayetano kissed her.

His wife. His Queen.

His.

And he had intended to set the necessary wheels in motion immediately, but something in the way she looked at him stopped him. Or maybe it was that blazing flame of possessiveness that moved in him. He didn't want to leave her.

It should have horrified him to think such a thing. It did.

"Everyone is dancing," she said, and he could see the delight on her face as she turned back toward the crowd.

And he didn't have it in him to stamp it out.

She looked around, lit up with wonder. Because the people were dancing, right where they stood. He took her hand, and led her to the courtyard, where the crowd cried and stamped, danced and cheered around them. Then he led her up onto the ramparts, so she could look out and see all the people lined up outside the castle. The flags waving, the cheers seeming to well up from the valley itself to scrape the sky above.

"You have not merely married me today," he told her. With a fierceness he should not have allowed. "You have set us free."

And once again she proved herself, because she took his hands in hers, fixed her gaze on his, and did not shrug the moment away. "I will do my best to be the Queen you told me I could be. A bridge between the royal family and this valley. Never a barrier."

And for a moment, standing there high above the valley, while his people danced out their jubilation and Delaney was still only his, something in him turned over.

He almost let himself wonder what would happen if he…put it off a day. This revolution that no one knew was coming. These announcements no one awaited. What if he pushed it back another week, maybe three? Surely everyone deserved a honeymoon, even the true King of a contested throne.

Especially when he'd already won. Everything now was the bitter details.

He saw his mother's face again, her eyes still so bright with resentment. The embodiment of bitterness when once upon a time, she had burned with a different kind of zealotry.

He would not succumb to the same temptations. He would not become the very thing he loathed.

But he couldn't seem to say the words. Not when Delaney was gazing at him the way she was now, her face so soft and yet her eyes so fierce. Not when everything in him clamored to wait. To hold her here. To sink into this moment.

To live for something else, if only for the night.

The treachery of that thought appalled him. He might as well be his parents all over again, giving lip service to the cause but in the end, only truly dedicated to their own selfishness. Was that what he wanted?

When he had come so far? When he had made vows to himself that he would never, ever risk his people in this way?

When he had been so sure that he would be better?

His own weakness sickened him.

"I must leave you," he told Delaney abruptly. Sternly, as if she'd tried to stop him. "There's much to do."

She looked startled. "Now? We have not been married an hour."

"My people have waited for centuries," he told her, sounding all the more disapproving because he felt much the same. "Surely they need not wait another moment."

His own gut twisted at that, because she didn't look angry. She looked hurt. But she looked away for a moment, and when she looked back her gaze was clear.

And he told himself that he had imagined it, that was all. For his Delaney was nothing if not practical.

"Of course," she said in her usual calm way. "You must do what is necessary, Cayetano. I understand."

And he didn't like how hard it was to walk away. He didn't like that when he found his ministers and they gathered together to begin this much-planned and plotted-out endgame, no small part of him wanted to turn around and go back.

The sound of his own wedding was loud inside the stone walls as the party raged on in the courtyard. And instead of feeling nothing but pride and determination as he trod up the steps that would lead him to the throne at last, he felt…a kind of hollowness.

He had no idea what to call it. No clue what it was. He had never encountered such a thing before.

Especially not when he should have been triumphant straight down to his bones.

But he encountered it a lot over the next weeks of work and strategy, worse every day until he admitted the unnerving truth.

He missed her.

Sometimes he missed her so much it neared the point of pain, but by the time he identified the problem, it was too late.

Because Cayetano had finally gotten what he wanted.

He had finally turned the Montaigne family rule on its head.

He had released news of his wedding first with the photographs of the two of them at the altar, looking, as one of his ministers liked to say, like love's young dream incarnate. He had used every media contact he'd ever made to sell the world a love story.

And the world had responded.

Loudly.

It turned out the story of a farm girl Cinderella and a throneless king caught the fancy of well-wishers the globe over. Their wedding photos appeared on the front covers of magazines and papers in too many countries to count. Delaney was an instant icon, a title she disliked intensely—but after a particularly enterprising paparazzo dug out a photo of her in her overalls, no retailer could keep them in stock. Anywhere.

Talking heads in a slew of languages discussed her *eclectic style,* from comfortable overalls to her fairy-tale gown.

"They talk of your gravitas and they wonder what undergarments I wear," Delaney said one morning as they watched some of the coverage in his office, too many ministers about for it to be anything like the private moment Cayetano craved. "I'm sorry, but how is this a ringing endorsement?"

"It's spin," his media guru said shortly. "We want people to look up to the warlord. We want them to imagine they *are* you."

Delaney smiled politely back at the man and murmured her thanks.

Cayetano, for some reason, wanted to kill him.

He refrained.

And he waited until his first in-depth, televised interview, with Delaney at his side, to drop the bomb of her parentage.

"Imagine my surprise to discover that this perfect woman is also the true heir to the Ile d' Montagne throne," he said, as if he had happened upon Delaney on her farm and had then uncovered her parentage. He had not lied about how they met. He had simply not explained it.

Delaney laughed a bit ruefully, looking

straight into the cameras. "Imagine mine," she said dryly.

And the world's love affair turned into sheer adoration.

While Cayetano sat back and let the debris fly where it would.

At first it was nothing short of a tempest. It blew and blew, and it was hard to tell if he was exhilarated by the intensity of the storm or if he wanted to it to die down. Maybe both.

It went on and on. Tests upon tests were demanded, laboratories were questioned, more tests were required. Emissaries from the Montaignes exchanged bitter words with the Arcieri representatives, and vice versa. But eventually, all the storming about in the world had to give way to the inescapable truth.

Especially in the glare of so much attention. And Delaney's rising popularity.

"I have been personally summoned to Palais Montaigne," Delaney told him one day. He had been up late the night before strategizing, and had found her in their bed, asleep. She had woken when he'd stretched out beside her and they'd come together the way they did so often these days. Wordless. Desperate.

It was never enough.

Cayetano found himself missing those weeks before the wedding, when the days had seemed to last forever and the nights twice as long. He had explored her body in every possible way, yes, but they had also had time to sit together. Sometimes he had held her in his lap, wrapped up in a blanket as they'd sat out on the balcony, telling each other silly, throwaway things while the moon rose above them.

He had never expected to miss anyone the way he missed her now, even when she stood before him.

The way she did today, and he felt another pang, for there was no sign left of his farm girl. He hadn't been able to get rid of those overalls quick enough, the world was obsessed with them, and now he found himself missing them, almost. Because this Delaney was almost *too* polished. This was the Delaney who sat beside him in interviews and sounded cultured. Sophisticated. Royal. No trace of Kansas about her.

Today she was dressed in one of her uniforms, a quietly elegant A-line dress in a bright shade that complemented her coloring. Nothing too flashy. Nothing off-putting. Her hair was styled to casual perfection as it fell around her shoulders. She sat in his office with her usual self-possession, as if she hadn't noticed that they only really talked here, now.

She had long since far exceeded even his most optimistic hopes for her.

He had made a farm girl into the perfect princess.

Cayetano should have felt nothing but joy at his success.

And yet.

"I am not surprised that the Montaignes finally wish to see you in their lair," he said, trying to focus on the matter at hand, not these strange and unwelcome *feelings* that seemed to pounce on him at odd hours. These bizarre emotions he would have said he was immune to, for he always had been before. "They have tested and retested your blood. And Princess Amalia's. And Queen Esme's, too. It's only been a matter of time."

Once again, he thought he saw a glimpse of something too dark in her gaze, but it was gone in the next breath.

"Time has run out, apparently," she said in the same steady way she said everything these days. He found himself recalling that brash, awkward girl who had blurted out her innocence at his table.

That version of Delaney seemed like a dream he'd had.

"It is an invitation to private dinner with the Queen," she told him. "Family only. She has not mentioned you specifically, but I'd prefer it if you came."

"She's testing you." Cayetano sat back in his chair and wished his wide desk was not between them. "She wishes to see for herself how ambitious you are."

Delaney frowned and he was so pleased to see it—a *frown*, for God's sake—that it was unseemly.

"What does ambition have to do with an awkward family dinner?" she asked.

"An ambitious woman would come without her husband," Cayetano told her smoothly, but he was more focused on the novelty of seeing her frown at him to worry that she was that sort of woman. "And dedicate herself to making an ally of the Queen instead." He considered her for a moment. "Is that what you wish to do?"

Delaney shrugged, and something in him eased, because it was the shrug of that girl he'd found in Kansas, not the perfect princess he crafted here. He did not care to examine how relieved he was to see she was still in there. "I don't really see the point. She is not young. And whether she and I are allies or not will not matter in the end, will it?"

He found himself smiling at her. At that relentless practicality. "As you say."

But then his ministers were at the door again,

Delaney excused herself, and it was another late night of giving interviews to different time zones. And once again he found her sleeping when he made it to their bedroom. This time she did not wake, so he lay down beside her and waited for sleep to claim him.

And found himself wondering why it was that now, having gotten what he wanted in every possible way, he had never felt more alone.

Come morning, Cayetano was appalled at his own mawkishness. He punished himself with a brutal training exercise with his guards, then prepared himself for the showdown he'd been anticipating for most of his life.

Tonight he would face Queen Esme. And not as a rebel, but as the man who would take back her throne. But first, he took himself to see the other woman who'd influenced his life beyond measure.

His mother.

Her lover, his would-be stepfather, had left the country after Cayetano had defeated him in combat. His mother could have taken that option, but had chosen to remain instead. Even though he would only allow her to do so under supervision.

"Call it what it is, Cayetano," she said this day the way she always did. She lit herself one of the long cigarettes she favored—as much because he disliked them as anything else, he assumed. "The mighty warlord has kept his mother in jail while he makes a run at the throne. How proud you must be."

"Soon you will be as free as the rest of us," he told her, deliberately bland. Because he knew how to annoy her, too. "Tonight I dine with Queen Esme. I have already married her true heir. The deed is done, Mother."

His mother blew out a plume of clove-scented smoke. "A lost princess, switched at birth." She shook her head. "It's like something out of a storybook."

"It's science," he replied.

"Yes, yes, your precious facts," she murmured in her raspy way. Dismissively, as ever.

And when Cayetano looked at her, he hated the part of him that was still her son. The part that was only her son, and still wished she'd been less…angular. Less ambitious. Less about power and more about him.

But he had found the lost Princess of Ile d'Montagne. A man could not ask for too many miracles. It became greedy.

"I know facts are not your friends," he said. "I came here to inform you, that is all. Because however perverse, I know that at one time, you were focused on the same enterprise."

"I wanted to cut them all down," his mother said, her eyes glittering with what he assumed was remembered fury. "As they deserve."

"You wanted to take my place," he corrected her. "Violent solutions were the excuse, not the reason."

She laughed at that, but it was not a good sound. "I pity your princess."

This was his cue to leave. He knew that. Therese liked nothing more than to poke at him. It was all nonsense and malice that he usually shrugged off as he left. But when it came to Delaney, he couldn't help himself. He couldn't let it go.

"My princess reclaims her rightful place in the world," he informed his mother. "She does so with grace and sensitivity, unlike some I could mention. She met with Princess Amalia only last week and came away the stronger for it. Save your pity for yourself."

It had been a stiff, formal meeting, entirely staged for the cameras to assuage the international interest in the story of babies swapped at birth. The sort of interest Cayetano had always craved, and yet now it was happening, he found he liked it less than he should. It was that hollowness again. But all the tests were in, and conclusive, so the meeting of the two had gone forward. And it had been a strange farce of two similar-looking women, smiling as if their lives hadn't been upended, shaking hands and then sharing a tea service while scrums of journalists hung on their every stiff and overly polite word.

Still, Delaney had told him later, *at least our first meeting is over. It was almost better that there was no chance to talk about anything.*

"She loves you," his mother said now. "It is painfully obvious. And as we know, you are your father's son. You care only for facts and figures, plots and plans. But nothing at all for the emotions that make any of this worthwhile."

He restrained himself from rolling his eyes, but barely.

"You will be set free from your remarkably comfortable prison just as soon as Queen Esme issues the proclamation we've all been waiting for. An announcement of the new line of succession. If I were you, I would take the time to reflect on the fact that you have not been, as you like to claim, imprisoned for *love*. But rather because you attempted a coup. Let us be honest about that, Mother, please. If nothing else."

He expected the cloud of smoke she blew his way. Sometimes she even threw things at him. But she surprised him by sighing.

"I loved him," his mother said, far more quietly than usual. "I can admit it blinded me. But I loved him. And a love like that, no matter how it ends, is worth anything. Even this." She blinked, and the bitterness he knew best crept back over her face. "You'll never know that, Cayetano. Because you are precisely how you were made. Cold and cruel and destined to be alone forever."

That wouldn't have insulted him a month or two ago. He would have taken it as a compliment. But things were different now.

"If I'm cruel," he gritted out at her, "you have only yourself to blame. For I think you'll find that it's a natural response to a coup attempt. By a mother to her son. No matter how much you dress it up and try to call it a love story."

"Alone," his mother said, distinctly. "Forever."

And Cayetano spent the rest of his afternoon trying to get her voice out of his head.

With little success.

He worked up until the car arrived to take them down from the valley to the sea, where Palais Montaigne had stood almost as long as Arcieri Castle. Almost.

He fielded the usual calls as they wound through the mountains, aware that Delaney was beside him with her face turned toward the glass.

"Are you excited for tonight?" he asked, tossing his mobile aside.

She turned toward him, and he was struck, as ever, by her beauty. By the way she glowed. She looked almost ethereal, in a sparkling gown that made her look as if she, perhaps, was made entirely of froth and sparkling wine. She wore jewels around her neck that had been handed down in his family through the centuries, including the ring on her finger, the pride of many Arcieri brides before her.

Her expression was perfectly placid but still, there was something about the way she regarded him that made him regret…everything.

Cayetano was unused to the feeling. He disliked it intensely.

"It's a formality, surely," Delaney was saying. "All your sources in her palace indicate that she will be making her announcement soon. Possibly even tomorrow."

"We do not need her proclamation," Cayetano agreed. "The laws of the island dictate that you will inherit the throne, whether she likes it or not."

"So it is done, then." Delaney's blue gaze moved over his face. "You have everything you've wanted, all this time."

And he had spent a great many years fighting. Hand-to-hand combat, martial arts, exercises like today's with his guards. All in preparation for a future that, as far as he had known, might include more coup attempts from his own mother, assassination attempts from Montaigne sympathizers, and who knew what else.

This way of winning was better than those dark imaginings that had preoccupied him for so long. But her tone of voice sent a finger of premonition down the back of his neck. "I'm sure she also wishes to speak with you." He kept his voice…careful. "She is, after all, your mother."

Something flashed in Delaney's gaze. "She is not my mother. I already have a mother."

Cayetano could hear the wealth of pain there. The hurt. The betrayal. He recognized all of it.

And for the first time in a long while, he found…he didn't know what to do.

He reached over and took her hand as he'd done before. He held it in his, though he could not have said, in that moment, if he sought to comfort her…or himself.

Delaney frowned down at her hand as if it wasn't connected to her. Or to him.

"You have everything you ever wanted," she said quietly. And before he could figure out how to answer that, though he registered the tone as dangerous but had no earthly idea why, she kept going. "But what do I have?"

Me, he wanted to say. But couldn't. Because he'd barely seen her since their wedding day. Because he had gone out of his way to make certain she had everything *but* him.

And he could spin any story he liked to anyone who asked. He did it all day long.

But he couldn't lie. Not to her. "Delaney."

Her fingers gripped his, but she lifted her gaze and it speared straight through him, pinning him to his seat.

"I love you, Cayetano," she said, but in a quiet way. A warning sort of way. "I thought you must know this, because why else would I spend twenty-four years perfectly happy to keep to myself only to fling myself into your arms with such abandon? I followed you across the world. I made myself into a princess when all I've ever loved is good, honest work in the dirt. For you."

He felt choked. He couldn't speak. It was as if there were hands tight around his throat, and he was fairly certain that if there were, they were hers.

"Little one," he began.

"I love you," she told him, with a little more intensity. "Even though you left me on our wedding day. Even though it is as if you've disappeared since."

"You knew what had to happen," he managed to grit out, and no matter that it sounded inadequate even to him now.

She smiled, but it was not that smile of hers that made the sun shine brighter. It hit him then that he didn't know when he'd last seen it.

And this one was sad. So deeply sad it broke his heart, when until this moment he would have sworn he didn't have one. That he'd lost it long ago.

That he had banished it the way he'd banished any hint of emotion within him.

The way he'd banished his own mother, too.

Cayetano didn't much care for the way that realization sat on him.

"I love you," Delaney again, her voice faintly scratchy now. "But all you love is this throne that you won't even have until an old woman dies. I love you, Cayetano. I do. But all things considered, I think I prefer the cornfields."

CHAPTER ELEVEN

DELANEY PROBABLY COULD have picked a better moment.

The car had nearly made it into the island's main city. Outside, the sun was heading toward the waiting sea, sending a lustrous golden light dancing over the white and blue buildings, interspersed with splashes of terra-cotta and covered in bougainvillea. As they made it further down the mountainside, the roads changed, too. Still winding and narrow, so unlike the wide-open roads where she'd been raised—but made treacherous in places by the curious spectators who'd come out to see if they could get a glimpse.

Of her. Of Cayetano.

Of the unexpected new future of their country.

She'd experienced the same thing on her way to her meeting with Princess Amalia, too. A meeting she would have put off forever, if it had

been up to her. But then, nothing was. She'd
handled the churning inside her by channeling
it into an intense interest in this part of the island, so different from up in the valley where
she had been treated more as a prize than a
curiosity.

Tonight she found herself scanning the different faces, looking through the different ex-
pressions. Much as she had when she'd been
unable to let herself think about her imminent
meeting with Princess Amalia. The real Clark.

And she had changed so much in her weeks
on this island. She had accepted that she was
holding on to Kansas in ways she shouldn't.
She had also accepted that falling in love with
Cayetano was an excellent way to avoid thinking about all the unpleasant family things that
still made her stomach twist.

She'd become okay with taking on the role
of Cayetano's queen.

It was the current Queen—and the woman
who'd expected to succeed her—that made her
feel off-balance again. One was her biological
mother. The other might as well have been a
blood relation, given how much they shared,
like it or not.

And the fact that it was only the two of them,
princess and farm girl, who could possibly understand what had happened to them.

What was still happening to them.

I'm told I come from a long line of farmers, Amalia had said, smiling brilliantly over her tea. *How splendid. It sounds significantly more honest than royalty.*

Delaney had seen behind the smile. She'd seen the darkness lurking there. The confusion. She'd felt it herself.

Less treacherous, I think, she had replied. *But still, I wouldn't turn your back on the chickens.*

Amalia had laughed, and then looked as if the sound surprised her. *Never fear,* she'd said briskly. *I don't think that will be a problem.*

Because she likely had as much interest in farming as Delaney had initially had in princessing. And yet despite herself, Delaney had liked the other woman tremendously.

Liking Amalia felt like the one thing that was hers. There was no betrayal involved. No giving up anything. They had been switched at a hospital when they were days old. If that didn't forge a bond, Delaney couldn't imagine what could.

On the drive back, she had found herself even more aware of the gawkers. Lined up to stare, to make up stories, to tell lies—and she'd told herself to get used to it. This was her life now. This bizarre fishbowl.

That day, she'd told herself it was worth it, because she had Cayetano.

Everything in her had changed so profoundly after that first night. Once she had let go of what remained of her old identity, she found she knew herself better than she ever had before. Part of it was him in all his *dark glory*. But part of it, she thought now, was what Catherine had been trying to tell her.

It had been what she'd been attempting to explain Cayetano about carrying a burden.

If he hadn't found her, she never would have thought of the farm as a *burden*. It brought her as much joy as it did struggle, even if the fight to keep it going had seemed to take more out of her each year.

She hadn't known how to let go of that. She'd never planned to let go. And she never would have, on her own.

The choice been taken from her and that night, she'd accepted it.

Just as she'd accepted him into her body.

And for a time, she'd truly believed that was enough. It had felt like more than enough in those first days. She'd imagined that what they were building together would bloom. That it would last.

But everything had changed on their wedding day.

Maybe it was one too many betrayals.

"I don't know what you want from me," he said from beside her now, and when she glanced at him the look on his face seemed to scrape through her, leaving her raw.

She looked down at their hands, still joined. She wore his ring now, the ring he had not shown her himself because, of course, he'd never actually proposed. He'd left it in the care of the majordomo, who had told her, with great pomp and circumstance, the historical significance of the Arcieri diamond. Delaney had received a long lesson on the topic before the ring had been packed away, not to be seen again until Cayetano had slid it on her hand during their wedding ceremony.

Every night she slept in his bed. He usually woke her when he came to bed, later and later all the time. No matter how she tried to stay up, she always seemed to be asleep when he arrived, so her marriage so far seemed to her like little more than a fever dream.

Some parts of it were beautiful. She wouldn't deny that.

But none of it felt *real.*

"Are you threatening me already?" he continued when she did not respond. "Do you think there's any possibility I will let you leave, Delaney?"

And she wasn't sure when it had occurred to her that she couldn't leave. Not because he would stop her, though he might. But because she didn't *want* to leave. She was too invested.

I never wanted to leave Kansas, she'd confessed to Catherine, who had been almost too understanding about not being present at her wedding. She'd laughed and said it was far beyond her to guess at the reasoning of royalty. *I never had the slightest desire to go anywhere.*

And now you have the whole world, Catherine had said with all her usual warmth, as if nothing had changed when everything had. *I'm so proud of you.*

As if she knew Delaney needed that courage. Because she'd always known.

"I don't think I said I was leaving," Delaney said now.

"Forgive me." His voice was scathing. "I must have misinterpreted your loving remarks about preferring cornfields to my company."

"Cayetano." She turned toward him, and faced him, there in the back of the car. The beautiful island was putting on a show in the syrupy gold of the coming sunset, but she couldn't focus on this place. Because what was this place to her without him? "I married you. You do know that for all your bluster, I didn't have to do that, don't you?"

"I know that is what you like to think."

He pulled his hand away and she wasn't surprised to see him curl it into a fist, there on his powerful thigh.

"I like to think it because it's true," she said, her voice no longer as steady as she would have liked. "You forget, I've met your people now. They would never have cheered as they did on our wedding if I had not looked happy. They would not have supported you if you had behaved the way they believe the Montaignes have behaved for so long. I might not have known that you were bluffing about forcing me into marriage at first, but after all these weeks, how can you imagine I haven't learned the truth?"

That hard, beautiful face of his changed again, until he looked less like the man she'd come to know. Less like the lover she knew so intimately now, there in the dark of their bed. Less like the leader he was in the eyes of his people, who would follow him anywhere, willingly.

"If you do not intend to try to leave me, I do not see the point of this conversation," he bit out as if this was one of his wars. "I never made any secret of the fact that our marriage must serve a purpose. I apologize if that purpose was not made clear to you, or if you did not understand what pursuing that purpose would entail. I will have words with the majordomo."

"I understand perfectly," she retorted. "And I think you know that your majordomo would hurt himself before he would neglect his duty."

It was amazing how much affection she'd come to have for that stuffy old man and his uniform. She would hear no word against him, not even from Cayetano.

Beside her, Cayetano nodded stiffly, so Delaney continued.

"I have no problem with the purpose. Our purpose. But I want more than a few stolen hours in the middle of the night." She waited for him to look at her, his burnt gold eyes nearly dark now. So dark she had to repress a shiver. "I want everything, Cayetano. I want a real marriage. I don't see why our marriage can't be like the weeks that preceded our wedding."

"Because they cannot," he bit out, and the anguish that streaked through his gaze took her breath. "It can never be like that again. You wouldn't like it if it was."

"I don't understand," she began, though a trembling sort of uncertainty had taken up residence inside her, and surely this time, touching him wouldn't help. No matter how much she wanted to. "Cayetano, surely—"

But he sat forward, cutting her off that easily. She had started taking lessons in French and Italian, but her few hours of wrestling with two new languages wasn't enough to understand his rapid-fire instructions to the driver. She sat there, her head spinning, as the driver turned off the main road, followed a few side streets, and then headed back into the hills. But instead of taking the road that led back toward the valley, when they reached the spine of the mountain, the car went the other way.

"Where are we going?" she asked. Softly.

Almost as if she didn't want to know.

Cayetano didn't answer her. He only shook his head, staring out the window with that telltale muscle tense in his jaw.

Delaney blew out a breath, then directed her gaze out the windows, too. The car followed the narrow, twisting road that wound its way along what was nearly the very top of the mountain. It was an undeniably stunning drive, though she doubted very much that Cayetano had been seized with the sudden urge to take her sightseeing. Still, they were so high up that Ile d'Montagne looked like something out of a storybook. On one side of the car there were views into the beautiful valley she'd come to love so much these last couple of months. And on the other, down the slope the outside of the mountain, picture-perfect villages nestled with the sparkling, beckoning sea beyond.

She wished she could appreciate it all the way she wanted to, but her pulse was hammering at her. And Cayetano seemed farther away than he ever had been before. It made her stomach twist.

The car pulled out onto a kind of overlook, then stopped. For moment, nothing happened. Delaney snuck glances at Cayetano beside her, but he looked as if he really had turned to stone. Only that clenched fist and the muscle in his jaw gave him away.

After some time had passed, his nostrils flared. Then he threw open the door beside him and got out.

Delaney took a breath or two, gave up trying to do something about her drumming heart, and then followed him.

It was windier up this high, and she was acutely aware of the foolish clothes she was wearing—all dressed up tonight to meet the current Queen. At first they'd felt like bizarre costumes, these dresses. But the Signorina had helped her feel at ease in them. She had taught Delaney to dance in them. And more than that, had encouraged her to run through the halls of the castle, play, walk outside, and fling herself messily on this couch or that as it moved her.

Until Delaney no longer felt as if her chattering trio was dressing a mannequin—a mannequin who wasn't her—every time she dressed for one of her events.

But here, on this rocky outcropping with such a steep drop below, the sun dripping toward the horizon and the sea all around them like a deep blue halo, all she could think about was the absurdity. This dress with its silly ruffles and shoes better suited for circus, they were so much like stilts, as she wandered around this island playing princess games.

Yet it was an absurdity she had come to appreciate.

All because of the man who stood at the edge of the overlook, staring out into the distance.

She had the stray thought that she wished she could jump back in time to show herself who she'd become, because she knew the old version of Delaney would have laughed herself sick at the very idea.

But even as she thought that something in her rejected it.

The old Delaney was gone now. She was *this* Delaney now. Princess Delaney, the papers were already calling her. And there was no possible way she could ever go back. Cayetano was a huge part of that, but it was more than simply him.

She had gone too far from Kansas to ever imagine she could sink back into the life she'd left there. Delaney understood that she would no longer fit.

And maybe that was why, though her heart kicked at her and her stomach cramped, she was able to go and stand beside Cayetano, there at the edge. And remain calm, though the height was worrying and the look he threw her way was something like ravaged.

For a time there was nothing but the wind, and the sun painting the sky in oranges and pinks as it sank.

"I cannot allow myself to love," he told her at last, in the ringing tones he'd used long ago, there in the yard at the farm.

This time, she didn't laugh.

Though she was sorely tempted, if only for symmetry.

This time, she considered what he'd said for a moment, then sniffed. "That seems stupid," she replied, calmly. Very, very calmly. "If you want my opinion."

He turned to look at her fully then, and it wasn't that she was immune to how tormented he looked. He tugged at her the way he always did, and the way, she imagined he always would. It hurt her to see him hurt. She supposed that was what loving someone did.

But Delaney hoped she loved him enough to hold out for better than this. For more. From both of them.

Love isn't a weak little greeting card on a holiday, Grandma Mabel had told her, long ago, when elementary school aged Delaney had not received any valentines on Valentine's Day one year. *Love is ferocious. It is fearless. It is not for the faint of heart, child. It takes a warrior.*

And Cayetano was a warlord. But Delaney was prepared to be a warrior, now, when it was needed.

Whenever it is needed, she promised herself. *As long as we're together.*

She had to hope that she wore her fearlessness on her face.

Maybe she did, because at last, Cayetano began to speak.

"My father was not a cruel man," he told her, as if the words hurt him. "But he was distant. Focused. It was always clear that he had married and had a child because it was expected of him, not because he had any emotional investment being a husband or father. I was never sure if he had any emotions at all. My mother would tell you he never did."

"I'm sorry," Delaney said softly, trying to imagine growing up like that. "It can't have been easy to be the son of such a man."

"You misunderstand," Cayetano bit out. "His focus was the cause. Our people were his only concern and nothing else mattered to him. He was a hero."

He rubbed his hands over his face, and Delaney wanted, badly, to reach over and touch him. But something stopped her.

"He died when I was twelve," Cayetano said, his gaze out toward the setting sun again, all that golden light spilling over the harshness of his expression. And it was as if she could feel that same harshness inside her, like so many jagged edges, cutting into her. Making her ache. "I was in boarding school in England, so it fell to my guards to tell me. They pulled me out of class, sat me down, and called me *warlord*. I was not permitted to fly home. It was thought that having me at the funeral was a risk too great."

"That's terrible," Delaney whispered, and had to grip her own arms as she hugged them close to keep from reaching for him.

"On the contrary." He looked down at her from his great height, stern and something like ruthless—though his eyes were dark. Too dark. "My father's death is what made me. I had no choice but to jettison my emotions. My guards made it clear to me that I was the face of Ile d'Montagne, then and always. That any outbursts on my part would not only reflect badly on my people, but would be trotted out as evidence to show that the House of Montaigne's possession of the throne that was rightfully mine was warranted. Even at twelve I was keenly aware that I could not let that happen. No Arcieri has been born in centuries without accepting that it was more than likely that his attempts to regain the throne would fail. I never expected to win it back, Delaney. But I would die before I made the situation worse."

Delaney could feel the ache in her grow sharper. Those edges dug in harder.

But Cayetano kept going. "It was not until years later that I understood the truth of what happened to him. It was a car accident. Here." Delaney jolted at that, and the way he slashed his hand the air, harsh and hard. "My mother, always the emotional one, had been in a rage. She wanted his attention. As ever, his focus was on bringing our people's case to the world, the better to put pressure on Queen Esme. They had a blazing row and my father took off from the castle, leaving his guard behind and driving himself to his death. They say he lost control of the car here. Because he was not perfect. He was cold and slow to anger, but when his temper finally engaged, it was catastrophic. He proved it so."

Now Cayetano was breathing hard, as if he was running. His gaze was so dark that it, too, began to hurt her as he stared down at Delaney.

"Do not apologize," he growled when she opened her mouth to do just that. "He was reckless, in the end. For all his focus, all his disinterest, he let emotions get the better of him and he lost control of his vehicle. He was a leader of men. A hero to the cause. He should have known better."

She heard the bleakness in his tone. And all she could do was whisper his name.

"But instead, he died." Cayetano looked desolate. Stark stone carved in unforgiving lines. "And that left my mother, in all her erratic sentimentality, in charge until I came of age. I know you read up on my family. I'm certain you know what this moment of recklessness cost us all."

Delaney had read the dispassionate facts of his life on the first night, after he'd showed up out of nowhere. But it was something else again to hear him tell it. And she hadn't loved him then—she'd merely been fascinated against her will. Now that she loved him with everything she was, all she could think was of the boy he'd been, caught in all these terrible forces so much larger than himself.

Not even allowed to grieve.

"She fell in love again, she claimed." Cayetano's voice was derisive. "Then she and her lover schemed to take what was not theirs. I was forced to fight him, with my hands, to claim what was already mine. And none of this would have happened if either one of my parents could truly control their emotions."

Her pulse picked up at that. She reached out, then dropped her hands before she made contact. All she could do was whisper his name again, as if maybe—if she said it the right way—he would hear her.

"I know what love is, Delaney," he told her. Mercilessly. "I know what it does. And I decided a long time ago that I would never allow it in my life. You will have to live with that."

And that should have cut her in two. She imagined it was meant to. She could see the recklessness he'd accused his father of in his gaze then, and on some level, she understood it.

He thought that if he hurt her enough, it would save him from what he must have spent all these years believing was his fate. But she knew better than most that fate was only fate until perspective shifted.

Until the truth was told.

"No," she told him, clearly. Her gaze steady on his. "I don't have to live with that. And I won't."

"I won't love you," he threw at her, as if this

was a fight and he had to respond with every last bit of rage and anguish within him. "I can't."

"Cayetano," she said, with all the certainty of the ferocious heart in her chest, "I think we both know you already do."

And she watched as something immense slammed into him. It was as if she'd taken some kind of sledgehammer to the top of his head, cracking open the armor that surrounded him so that the light trapped inside poured out.

So much light that it rivaled the sunset.

He looked dazed. Then he surged forward, taking her upper arms in his hands and lifting her up to her toes.

"It is a death sentence," he growled at her. "Or a lifetime imprisonment in a cell of your own making. That's what love would do for you, Delaney. Is that what you want?"

"I want you," she threw back at him, letting herself blaze in turn. "All of you. If that ends badly, Cayetano, maybe we deserve such a terrible fate. For not loving enough. For not loving well. For letting all the rest of this twist us into pieces."

He shook his head. His grip tightened, but she melted against him and slid her palms on his chest. He was hot, hard. He was mouthwatering. He was Cayetano.

And he was hers.

Whether he knew it or not.

"I promise you that I will love you more than enough, and well," she told him then, and this time, she could see that he was riveted to these vows she made. Unlike the ceremony in the courtyard. "I will put you first. Before crowns and thrones, the reporters who follow you around, the lies people tell. Your heart and my heart, Cayetano. And what we build together. That's what I love. That's what I want. All of you." She slid her right hand up to cover his heart and held it there as she felt it pound. "And all of me. Forever."

He looked haunted. Ravaged straight through. She could see the storm that worked in him, and she almost thought she could hear it, too, like thunder everywhere.

Inside and out.

But she was from Kansas. No storm could scare her.

When he spoke, it was to whisper her name. Again and again, like a melody.

"I don't know how to do this," he told her, when the storm had faded into song, and only the thunder of his heartbeat remained.

Still, she held his gaze. She reminded herself that she was a warrior. Fearless and ferocious.

"Do you want to?" she asked quietly. "All you have to do is *want* to love me. We can build anything we like from there."

It seemed to her then that the golden sunlight of the last of this day…changed. That it fell across him in a new way. Or maybe it was simply the way he looked at her, something so raw and intense in his gaze she wasn't certain how she could ever look away.

His hands moved on her arms, smoothing up, then down. Then he let out a ragged breath, that she knew, without doubt, was as close as this man of granite ever came to a sob.

"I want to," he whispered, his eyes dark with longing and need, and his voice rough. "Delaney… I want nothing more."

She felt moisture threaten the backs of her eyes. But she moved closer, tipping her face up so she could be closer to him. So she could see all of him.

Because he was still and always the most beautiful thing she'd ever seen.

"That was the hard part," she promised him. "Everything else is downhill."

Cayetano shifted so he could hold her face between his hands.

"I'm not afraid of hard," he told her, his eyes blazing gold once more. "Or hills. But I could not live with it if we do to each other what my parents did. If we even come close."

Delaney lifted her hands to cover his. "We get to decide. We get to choose. Destiny might have brought us together, Cayetano, but it doesn't get to decide how we stay together." Her voice was fierce. Her gaze was steady on his. "We get to choose how we live."

He made a low sort of noise, like something in him was broken. And then he was kissing her, all the heat and dark glory, all that raw desire.

But today it was so much more.

Today, it was laced through with hope.

"I will make you happy," he told her, resting his forehead on hers as the setting sun finally made it to the sea. "I will do my best, every day. And I will love you, Delaney. I love you now—I think I loved you at first sight, overalls and all. I promise I will love you with all that I am. And I cannot promise you that it will always look the way you wish it to. I cannot promise you that it will be the way you imagine it. But I do promise you that I will always try. So that somehow, between us, we will achieve something I have long thought was nothing more than the story. A silly little fairy tale."

"But you and I are made to do impossible things, Cayetano," Delaney said, and her tears fell freely even as she smiled. So wide she thought she could rival horizons. "You found a lost princess who shouldn't exist. You took back the throne of Ile d'Montagne after all these years. What's happy ever after next to that?"

He kissed her again, all that heat, and all of

it hers. Then he held her close as if he would never let her go.

She believed, at last, he never would.

"The happy ever after is everything, Delaney," he told her, the way some men said vows in churches. But this was their church, so high above the island they would rule together one day. This was who they were and who they would become, as long as they had each other. "You will see."

"Everything," she agreed, and the word felt like a brand, stamped deep into her skin.

Cayetano held her close as the sun sank below the horizon. As the old day ended so a new day could dawn.

But first, the riot of the stars, inside them and out.

Tonight it felt like they were filled with them.

"Everything," Cayetano repeated as the rest of their lives began. "And I promise you, my little farm girl, it will be ours."

And then, together, in the kingdom they cared for and the children they raised, they made it happen.

Until forever seemed like not nearly long enough.

CHAPTER TWELVE

CAYETANO ARCIERI WAS a man of his word.

They never made it to see Queen Esme that day. Instead, Cayetano took his wife back home, marinated in her, and the following day, set off on a long honeymoon that in no way made up for the first stretch of their marriage.

But he hoped it was a harbinger of the joys to come.

And as months became years, and hope became truth, he liked to think that they'd built the foundation for all that would come in those eight weeks.

Because with such a foundation, anything was possible.

Delaney and Queen Esme met, and while no one would describe them as *fast friends,* they found a way forward. Eventually, their way forward involved Catherine, too.

And years later, when time began to dull the edges of old memories, he found his way back to his own mother, too. Therese left Ile d'Montagne and married her long-lost lover, and Cayetano could see that truly, they loved each other.

Though even when his mother and he found ways to sit in peace together, speaking of soft and uncomplicated things, he made sure to make it clear that their love was better blooming off the island.

"I am far too old and tired to play games with your throne, Cayetano," Therese would tell him.

"Good," he would reply.

And the more time passed, the more they laughed.

But none of it would be possible if there hadn't first been those two sweet months, just Cayetano and Delaney.

No causes, no people. Just the two of them and that farmhouse in Kansas. Walking the land. Tending to vegetables, listening to the wind in the corn, getting dirty beneath the sun and lying out at night to lose themselves in the stars.

Most future kings did not honeymoon on a remote Kansas farm, but then, Cayetano was not most kings. He intended to be the best King Ile d'Montagne had ever had. He meant to split his time between the sea and the mountains. He meant to make his people whole.

A prospect that was only possible because he had Delaney.

He never took her for granted again.

Like all the things he studied, once he'd decided to love her he threw himself into it, body and soul.

"I love you," he liked to tell her when he woke her in the mornings, even years later, whether they were in their winter palace on the water or their summer castle in the hills. "I love you, little one. More today than yesterday."

Every day it was true.

"I love you, too," she would reply, always with that beautiful smile, wrapping herself around him while the morning sun danced in and the island breezes murmured all around them.

The way they'd woken up every morning of that honeymoon, tucked away beneath the eaves in that old farmhouse.

And he took care to love her there, when it was just the two of them. Deeply. Thoroughly. Before their children came bursting in. Before the concerns of the day took hold. Before they became King and Queen again.

First, they loved each other.

Fierce and ferocious, just Cayetano and Delaney.

Forever.

Just the way he'd promised.

* * * * *